Not Just Proms & Parties

Chelsea's Ride

Published by Lobster Press™
1620 Sherbrooke Street West, Suites C & D
Montréal, Québec H3H 1C9
Tel. (514) 904-1100 • Fax (514) 904-1101 • www.lobsterpress.com

Publisher: Alison Fripp
Editors: Alison Fripp & Meghan Nolan
Editorial Assistant: Molly Armstrong
Cover Design: Audrey Davis & Jenn McIntyre
Graphic Design & Production: Tammy Desnoyers

We acknowledge the financial support of the Government of Canada through the Book Publishing Industry Development Program (BPIDP) for our publishing activities.

The Canada Council for the Arts | Le Conseil des Arts du Canada

We acknowledge the support of the Canada Council for the Arts for our publishing program.

Library and Archives Canada Cataloguing in Publication

Penny, Patricia G., 1953-
Chelsea's ride / Patricia G. Penny.

(Not just proms & parties)
ISBN-13: 978-1-897073-44-5
ISBN-10: 1-897073-44-5

I. Title. II. Series: Penny, Patricia G., 1953- Not just proms & parties.

PS8631.E573C43 2006 C813'.6 C2006-900657-1

Printed and bound in Canada.

BLP

YA F PEN
1406 8756
Penny, Patricia G., 1953-

To Doris, Jane, and Karen who all believed.
And to RPG for being you.

– Patricia G. Penny

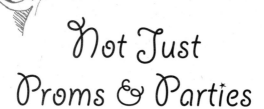

Not Just Proms & Parties

Chelsea's Ride

written by
Patricia G. Penny

Lobster Press ™

Chapter 1

Denny Waddell. Bad clothes, bad hair, bad skin. And he had the hots for Chelsea.

To make it worse, whoever designed the old brick house Chelsea lived in had made a huge mistake. The only bathroom was located off the front entranceway, right next to the front door, with a window that looked out onto the front porch. Denny had been out there for a while now, ringing the doorbell every few minutes and knocking on the door in between. She couldn't believe how persistent he had become.

The bathwater was getting cold. Chelsea was going to have to get out of it eventually or she'd catch pneumonia. Luckily she had lowered the blinds before undressing and settling in for a nice relaxing soak. Still, he must have seen that the light was on in the room, or he would have left by now.

She stretched her legs, caught the plug between her big toe and the next, then pulled until it popped up and the water started to drain. Standing, she grabbed a bright-colored towel from the rack beside the tub and wrapped herself quickly, as if Denny might be able to see through the blinds. She rubbed herself down awkwardly and climbed out of the tub to stand on the soft mat in front of the sink.

It was a few minutes since he had knocked. Maybe he had finally left.

She stepped off the mat onto the cold tile and leaned toward the window. Cautiously, she pulled back on a horizontal blind slat and peered behind the edge to survey the porch. *Crap!* He was there, sitting on a woven lawn chair and reading the *Sports Illustrated* that her father had left on the table. She angrily dropped the blind back into place and stormed out of the bathroom to the front door.

"What do you want?" she demanded of Denny as she pushed open the door. He looked up in surprise and then smiled slowly as he took in her towel-wrapped body and her wet hair clinging to her bare shoulders. She held the edge of the towel tightly in her grip to ensure that it stayed; if there was *anyone* who *wasn't* going to see her naked, it was Denny Waddell.

"Hey! I *thought* you were home. I saw you go into that room about an hour ago," he said as he pointed to the bathroom window. He stood up and came toward the door but stopped when he saw her hazel eyes flash at him.

"What, are you stalking me now?" It wouldn't surprise her. He was weird enough to do that.

"No, I was just driving by." *Fat chance.* Denny lived nowhere near her. She was grateful for that.

"So what do you want?" she asked again, holding the edge of the front door against her side so that she was deliberately blocking his way.

"I just wanted to visit you. Maybe see if

you want to hang out. Take in a movie or something. I don't know. Something."

He looked like a pathetic lost puppy. A mutt. One that had been running loose for a while and needed a good bath.

"I'm busy," she said, indicating the towel. "Maybe you've noticed I'm not dressed. Did you ever think that I might be tied up?"

He shrugged. "Sure. That's why I waited. I didn't want to interrupt."

A car pulled into the driveway and edged up beside his dated Chevy. The engine shut off and Chelsea's mother reached across the seat to grab her purse, then opened the door and climbed out.

"Hello," she said to Denny, seeming surprised but not too worried that a young man was standing at the door and talking to her daughter who was dressed in nothing but a bath towel. Chelsea could understand why her mother didn't look worried. No one looked less threatening than Denny.

"Hi. You must be Chelsea's mom," he said, walking across the porch with his hand outstretched.

"I certainly am." She smiled and shook his hand, looking over his shoulder at Chelsea with questioning eyes. She was probably thinking that this boy was not at all like the guys Chelsea was usually attracted to.

"I'm Denny Waddell," he informed her as he pumped her hand. "I'm a friend of Chelsea's."

Chelsea let out a short "hufff" and looked up to the sky for help. Maybe a higher power could explain what she had done to deserve this guy being at her house.

"Nice to meet you, Denny. Do you have a minute?" her mother asked.

"Sure. I don't have anything going on."

"It seems that Chelsea isn't dressed. I won't ask why that is. Maybe you could give me a hand with these groceries while she goes and gets some clothes on." She went to the back of the car and opened the trunk. Denny followed her down the two steps to the driveway and started reaching in to assist.

Chelsea huffed again and backed into the hallway, gripping her towel and closing the front door. She turned and scooted through the living room to the kitchen and then trotted up the stairs to the attic before they could come in the back door and see the view of her retreating backside.

Her bedroom was the only room up there. She had shared the tiny bedroom on the main floor with her younger sister, Leanne, until a couple of years earlier when her father had renovated the attic into a huge room for her. It was like a refuge, away from the rest of the family, away from everything. And right now, away from Denny.

She fell back onto her bed and the towel flipped open, exposing her shapely body. Ordinarily she wouldn't have cared. She had walked around naked in her room loads of times. But just knowing he was down there setting groceries on the kitchen counter gave her the creeps. She pulled the towel back across herself and rolled off the bed. She'd get dressed.

By the time she went back downstairs, her mother had put away all of the groceries and was sitting at the kitchen table having a cup of coffee with Denny. *Oh my God,* she thought to herself, *he's drinking coffee with my mother. He's infiltrated my home. He's like a flu bug.*

He smiled up at her innocently. The guy had no idea that he was a germ.

"Denny's going to stay for supper," her mother announced cheerfully. "We're having burgers and Caesar salad."

Chelsea gave her a look. She was usually pretty good at that, giving looks that could say "Hey! Great idea!" or "Are you out of your friggin' mind? Why did you do *that*?"

This look was definitely the latter.

Her mother didn't even seem to notice. She just went on sipping her coffee and asking Denny about school and his plans for college, as if he was the same as any other guy that Chelsea had brought home to meet her parents.

Chelsea felt her throat suddenly close and looked at them in horror. Her mother thought he was a *boyfriend! Eeewwww!*

"I have to go out later," she said quickly. "I've got a date." She didn't, but she'd take care of that.

"Oh," her mother answered pleasantly, probably thinking that Denny was the date, but it was obvious from his fallen face that he was disappointed to find out about Chelsea's announced plan.

"You can stay for supper anyway," Chelsea told Denny graciously. "You'll just have to leave right afterward. We're going to the early show."

"That's cool." He actually sounded as if he believed her. "What are you going to see? I really want to see that new one that just started, the one with Uma Thurman."

"Not that one," she assured him.

"I think you look a little like her. But prettier."

"Oh, that's so nice," her mother said, smiling at Chelsea and then back at Denny. It was one of those "oh, isn't that sweet" kind of looks.

"I don't look anything like her," Chelsea dismissed. "She has light blond hair for God's sake. And she has those eyes that are set too wide apart. I bet she can see cars coming up beside her without even using the side mirrors on her car."

He laughed as if it was the best joke ever, which made her immediately sure that it had been the worst joke ever.

"So who are you going out with?" he asked when he had stopped guffawing like a hyena.

"Oh, a few people." She'd have to call Jamal and see if he was busy. He was always a good sport. Maybe she could grab Sammy and Tara if they were free.

"Perhaps Denny would like to join you," her mother suggested. Chelsea looked at her with disbelief. Had the woman grown horns and a tail? Was she born in the god-damn bowels of the earth or something?

"No. No, Denny can't come." She could feel her face flushing. "Maybe another time. Not this time. We're, uh, pretty much committed to just the four of us going tonight. You know how Jamal is, kind of shy and all. He doesn't like a lot of people around."

In reality, Jamal was anything but shy. He had been a classmate and friend of Chelsea's for years. He had tried kissing her in the dark at the first 'boy-girl' party that they had ever been to way back when they were only thirteen. She had kissed him back and then told the other girls that he really could have used a mint. When he heard everyone laughing about it, he got back at her by saying he had copped a quick feel of her chest and that she had felt just like his brother. She responded by threatening to tell his mother that he smoked. He then promised to tell their teacher that she had cheated on the last two math tests. After that they had maintained a friendship borne of mutual respect and fear of what might come next if they *weren't* friends.

Jamal was like her; he poked fun at people outside their circle. He would understand about Denny. Jamal was as good an excuse as anything or anyone else she could come up with.

Denny and her mom were both looking at her silently. Her mother suddenly had a look of understanding followed by a half-amused smile that said she had finally gotten the message. Denny's face was just, well, Denny's face. She could have said that he had just won the lottery, or that his mother was a five-dollar hooker. He'd still be grinning at her the same way.

"I'll just start that salad then, so that we don't hold you up," her mother said.

"Leanne and your dad should be home from the library in a few minutes."

Chelsea murmured an excuse for going back upstairs and then made a few phone calls. She reached Jamal first and asked if he'd do her a favor and spend the evening with her.

"As a favor?" he asked suspiciously. "Why? Are you beyond bored or something?"

"It's Denny Waddell," she hissed into the receiver. "He's *here,* at my house, and I can't get rid of him. If I don't have other plans, then I'll *never* get rid of him."

"I would," he told her apologetically, "but I already have plans to go to my brother's place. He's having some guys over for poker."

"No! I really need you to do this for me, Jamal." Chelsea fell back onto her bed with a groan and resorted to pleading. "When do I ever ask you for anything? It's just this one time, please, please, please. I'll pay for the movie. I'll buy you popcorn. I'll ... I'll stand up and dance to 'YMCA' at the next school dance."

"Jeez, are you that desperate? Okay, I

guess I can just go to his place later. But trust me, I'll be making sure you do all the moves to that song. And I'll have them put a spotlight on you!"

"You're a lifesaver. I'm going to call Tara and see if she and Sammy can come."

She confirmed that they were free and then called Jamal back. "I'll try to get Mom's car and pick you up at 7:30. New terms. I've changed my mind about the 'YMCA.' I can't do it. But I'll buy you a pizza after the movie." And she hung up.

Later, Chelsea sat across the dinner table watching her sister serve salad to Denny Waddell, the creepiest guy in her school. He chatted animatedly with her parents and Leanne, looking over at Chelsea after every sentence and grinning like a gargoyle.. Chelsea ate as quickly as she could and then jumped up from the table to carry her dishes to the sink.

She heard Denny commenting on a black and white photograph he had noticed in their living room.

"I took that shot last year," her father said proudly. "I've taken a couple of photography courses."

"Me too!" Denny sounded excited to have found someone with a common interest. "I've got three cameras and my own darkroom."

"I always wanted to have a darkroom, but now, with a good digital camera and a high end printer ..."

"It's still nice to use the old Pentax single lens ..." Denny argued happily.

Chelsea snatched her empty salad bowl from the table and piled it on the other dishes noisily. She then took Denny's plate away before he could help himself to another hamburger.

This newfound link with her father was taking the situation from bad to worse. Now that Denny and her family seemed to be getting along so well, she wondered how she was ever going to get rid of him, and even more importantly, how she could keep him from ever coming back.

Chapter 2

As soon as her dishes were done and her excuses repeated, Chelsea snatched the car keys gratefully and left Denny at the kitchen table chatting with her parents. Ten minutes later, she was idling in Jamal's driveway.

"Whoa, Chels! They're letting you drive the Lincoln?"

Jamal climbed in the passenger side and sank into the leather seat. His dark hair was carefully styled and he was dressed in designer jeans and an Italian knit sweater over a collared shirt. He was a nice guy, but he always looked just a little too polished for Chelsea's liking.

"Mom is having some trouble with her brakes. She thought I'd better not drive her car until after she gets them checked out on Monday." She backed down his driveway with caution. The Lincoln felt huge and heavy compared to her mother's small car. "You look like you're dressed for church or something," she said to him.

"Sue me for trying not to look like Denny." He laughed in Denny's exaggerated chortle, and Chelsea rewarded him with her own easy laughter.

They picked up Tara and Sammy from Tara's house and drove to the multiplex theater by the mall. The movie they ended up watching was pretty stupid, but it got her away from Denny and that's all she had wanted. They left the theater and went to a restaurant downtown for the promised pizza. By the time she dropped Tara and Sammy off, it was just after midnight.

Chelsea drove the last few blocks to let Jamal out at his brother's house, where he assured her the poker game would just be getting into full swing. She waved as he headed inside without knocking and closed the door behind himself. A bare yellow bulb over the door shone in a jaundiced attempt to light the driveway. Yawning, she backed up and swung the Lincoln out onto the street. But she did it a little too quickly. Without checking her mirrors.

If the sound of glass breaking and metal scraping wasn't enough, she knew that she was in deep trouble when the back end of the car met with resistance at the side of the road. It didn't exactly hit something and stop with a jolt, the way it had when she had rear-ended a delivery truck last year. This time it felt as if it was pushing against something and maybe moving it a little. She jammed on her brakes and put the car into park. Her lights shone ominously up the deserted residential street.

Crap! Crap, crap, crap, crap, crap, crap, crap! She folded her arms across the steering wheel and banged her face down a couple of times on the softly-padded center of the wheel. *Crap! Stupid! Stupid, stupid, stupid, stupid!*

She sat up, took a deep breath, and stepped out of the car. The back right fender of the Lincoln was crushed up against the front left fender of a parked car. The Lincoln didn't look too bad. A small dent, some minor scratches. The other car, an older model with a huge hood, looked as if it had been hit with a Mack truck. The headlight was smashed, the fender caved in, the bumper folded under. *You are in deep shit, Chelsea, you idiot,* she thought to herself. *You are so dead. You're dog chow, girl.*

She looked at the house in front of which the car was parked. No lights were on. She glanced at the houses across the road. No lights anywhere. She looked back up the driveway to Jamal's brother's house. He was having a party, so she figured it must belong to someone there.

She left the car's lights on to warn people of the skewed position of her car, and started up the concrete path to the house. *Stupid people, parking on the road at night,* she thought. *Stupid streetlights, too far apart. Stupid Lincoln, so high you can't see past the back of it. Stupid me, stupid me, stupid me,* she repeated to herself as she rang the doorbell.

"Who owns the car that was parked too

close to your driveway entrance?" she demanded of the cigarette-smoking guy who answered the door.

"Chelsea?" Jamal came into the room and crossed over to where she stood as she challenged the guy, who appeared taken aback by her question. "What happened?" Jamal asked. He glanced over her shoulder toward the street and saw the Lincoln's lights shining along the boulevard. "Uh-oh."

"What am I supposed to do now?" she demanded, as though Jamal himself had parked a car in her way.

"Come on in," Jamal's brother answered, "and I'll tell Jay to go and take a look at his car."

Chelsea stepped into the hallway and followed Jamal and the other guy into the kitchen where a group of card players lost their best poker faces and forgot about their bets as they listened to the news.

"Aw, man! That better not be my car you're talking about." A heavy-set guy in his late twenties lay down his cards and pushed his chair away from the table.

Chelsea's anger gave way to dismay as

she saw the size of the man rising to his feet. He was big enough to play pro football. Defensive end. "It's just a small scrape," Chelsea said without conviction. She hoped that he didn't have a temper.

"It better be," he warned her, and his huge chest rose and fell as he pushed past her on his way to the door. "That's a reconditioned 1967 Roadrunner. It's an antique!"

Chelsea felt her chest tighten as she turned to follow him out the door. Jamal squeezed her arm in what she took to be a show of support and then followed her down the steps. *An antique*, she groaned inwardly.

"How bad can it be?" Jamal whispered to her. "You couldn't have been going very fast."

But a deep, agonizing groan followed by an unprecedented string of swearwords told Chelsea that the owner of the car knew a small scrape from a major fender bender. She winced and looked up to the clear night sky for help. She couldn't see any way out of this mess.

"I have insurance," she called out from the sidewalk to the huge man who was running his hand over the fender and talking to the car mournfully.

"Well, you'd better have a good policy," he snapped at her. "I should sue your sorry ..."

"Come on, man," Jamal interjected. "It was an accident. She messed up. We all make mistakes."

"Yeah, yeah. I hear you. But when I think of all the hours I put into restoring this car ..." the huge man moaned, shaking his head in disbelief.

Chelsea sighed and clutched Jamal's arm for support. "He thinks *he* has problems," she confided nervously. "He doesn't have to face my dad!"

* * *

"Never? What do you mean, *never*?" she asked her father in horror, after arriving home and explaining the night's events.

"It's your second accident in the one year you've been driving on your own. And you had that speeding ticket a couple of months ago. How many chances do you think we're going to give you?"

"But I *need* the car! How will I get

around? How am I going to get to work from school? How am I supposed to get to the library?" That last one was weak and she knew it. She hardly ever went to the library. *A girl's gotta try,* she thought.

He leaned forward in his chair and his eyes were resolute. "Do you have any idea how much our insurance is going to go up next year because of this? I'll be lucky if I don't have to change companies just to get insured at all. You will *not* be driving either one of our cars again. Period."

Chelsea looked at her mother for support, but she could see it was a lost cause. Her mother was looking at her as if she had just run over a nun or something.

"Frankly Chelsea, I think you're getting off lightly. Your father and I should make you pay for the difference in our insurance premium when it goes up. I don't think you fully appreciate just how serious this is."

"I didn't *try* to hit that car," she said, her voice starting to quiver. "It was an *accident*. He was parked in a bad spot and I couldn't see ..."

Her father stood up and started to leave

the living room. "We've heard enough Chelsea. Ride a bike, take a bus, walk." He was in the kitchen now, as good an indicator as any that he was done discussing it. He raised his voice so he could be heard from where he was. "Skateboard or roller skate around town if you have to. But you aren't ... going ... to drive ... our ... car!"

And just like that, Chelsea was without wheels. It felt as though someone had sentenced her to life in prison without days off for good behavior. Driving was her escape from the mundane existence of the Davison household. The car had been her ticket to a bustling social life, as well as a way of getting to work and practice. Life as she knew it would be over. Her social life would end. She'd become as dull as Leanne. And, she realized with horror, she'd be stuck at home where Denny Waddell was sure to find her.

"You're not being fair!" she yelled toward the kitchen, taking advantage of her father's distance to tell him how she felt.

"Chelsea! We have every right ..." Her mother's voice was sharp.

"And I don't have *any* rights! I get it!"

Chelsea stood and stormed out of the room, her head held high in a gesture of defiance. She ran up the stairs to her room and slammed the door for good measure. She hoped it would make them feel guilty for treating her like a child.

Throwing herself on the bed, she buried her face in her pillow. *I have got to find a way to get around,* she thought angrily. *If I can't drive, I'll go absolutely, positively crazy!*

Chapter 3

"I hear you totaled your dad's car over the weekend."

Chelsea looked up from her locker as she put her books away at the end of Monday's classes. Denny was leaning against the next locker and grinning at her. He was such a boxy, square, short, *duh* kind of guy. Who else but Denny would be grinning while talking to someone about a car accident?

"It was barely scraped," she said, grabbing her jacket from her locker and slamming the door shut with a decisive bang.

"I had an accident once," he announced, following her as she started down the hall. "I backed into one of those posts in the Wal-Mart parking lot. Put a big dent in my fender."

My God, she thought. He's trying to say we have something in common, something that will connect us more than just sharing a locker bay. *Eewwwww!*

"I fixed it myself. Just kind of tapped it back out from underneath. It looked pretty good. Didn't cost me a dime."

"Good going," she replied curtly.

"Maybe I could fix your dad's car. I wouldn't charge you anything. I'd just do it." Denny was trotting ahead of her a little, looking back at her with that puppy dog face, begging for the opportunity to do something for her.

"Dad already took it in to the dealership. They're just going to touch it up. It's the other guy's car that needs work. He's getting quotes on it. Then he'll take it in some place and the insurance company will pay for it."

He looked disappointed.

"Well, maybe next time."

"Next time? Do you think I get in accidents every day?" she turned to ask. "Why does everyone think I'm such a lousy driver?" She blew him off and started down the stairs to the front doors of the school.

"Well, let me know!" he called after her as she headed outside. "You know where I am!"

That's the problem, she thought as she strode toward the bus stop. *I know just where you are all the time.*

She checked her watch as she arrived at the bus stop down the block. There were a few other students waiting there as well, most of them noticeably too young to drive. One girl with a black tattoo of an ankle bracelet reached into her pocket and pulled out a loose cigarette and a package of matches. Chelsea met her eyes for a moment, watching as the girl lit up, inhaled, and then, with a challenging jut of her jaw, blew smoke directly into Chelsea's face before turning away. Chelsea was caught by surprise. She coughed on the smoke that she had involuntarily inhaled, then scowled at the girl blackly and moved a few steps away.

I knew it. Taking the bus is for losers, she thought. *And old ladies,* she added as she saw an elderly woman sit down on the bench next to the bus stop sign.

Chelsea checked her watch and frowned. She was supposed to be at work by 3:15 p.m. and it was already after three o'clock. If the bus didn't come soon, she would be late, and no matter how much she hated her job, she couldn't afford to lose it.

When the bus finally arrived, Chelsea followed the others up the black rubber steps and held out a five dollar bill to the driver.

"Exact change only," the driver said brusquely.

"What?"

"Exact change. A dollar twenty." He swung the door closed and edged out into traffic as Chelsea quickly grabbed the metal bar behind his seat to keep from falling over.

"I don't have exact change," she said, and heard one of the younger girls who had climbed on the bus before her start to giggle. She felt her face flush. *Who knew that taking a bus would be so complicated?* she thought.

"I'm not allowed to change bills. You should buy a bus pass," the driver advised as he stopped for a red light.

"I don't have the money to buy a pass right now," she confessed.

"I can't sell you one anyway. You have to get it at the depot between nine and five." He sounded bored. She wondered how many people got caught in this same situation every day.

"So what do I do now?" she asked, worried that he would force her off the bus at the next stop.

"Beg for change," he advised, tipping his head back toward the busload of riders who were observing her predicament with what could only be described as silent disinterest.

Chelsea felt her face start to burn as she looked at the riders on the nearly filled bus. She clutched her five dollar bill tightly and attempted to catch the eye of the fragile elderly woman who had so slowly climbed up into the bus just before her.

"Would you have change for a five?" Chelsea asked her hopefully.

The woman shook her head and smiled, exposing yellow teeth. "I don't carry much cash, dear. I use a senior's pass," she explained apologetically.

"Change?" Chelsea asked a young woman on the opposite bench. The woman put an arm around the child next to her and ignored Chelsea by looking out the window.

"Does anyone have change for a five?" Chelsea asked a little more loudly. She looked impatiently at the first few rows of people and waved the bill in the air. "A five? Anyone? Anyone?"

"Here," said the girl who had blown smoke in Chelsea's face earlier. She held a clenched fist out into the aisle and Chelsea moved forward thankfully to take the change. As she approached down the narrow aisle, the bus stopped suddenly and she stumbled, falling forward and almost landing in the girl's lap.

"Sorry!" she said with embarrassment, straightening herself and holding out the five dollar bill. The girl snatched it from her and dropped a pile of change into her hand.

"Thanks." Chelsea walked back up to the front and counted out the correct change, then dropped her money into the cash box. She glanced back down at her hand. Two dollars and sixty cents. The girl had stung her for a dollar twenty. She glanced back and saw the girl stare at her challengingly. Chelsea stared back to let her know that she could take her if she had to, then concentrated on just keeping her balance as the bus stopped and started along the busy route.

"Reid and Brookside," the driver called out a few minutes later. Chelsea moved to the back door and climbed off, appreciating the fresh air after the stale odor of the bus. She checked her watch again and started to run. She was three blocks from work and it was already after 3:15.

"I know, I'm late," she said, puffing as she opened the door to the chocolate shop where she had worked for the past month.

"What happened?" Verna asked her from behind the counter. Verna was the owner of the store. Chelsea knew she was a kindly woman with a big heart, but business was business, and Chelsea had clearly been told when she was hired that timeliness was important. She saw Verna looking at her from over the top of her glasses.

"No car," she gasped. "I have to take the bus now and it was late."

"Well, hurry and get into your costume. I won't dock your pay *this* time," Verna warned, and went back to refilling the display case with vanilla cream chocolates.

* * *

Chelsea worked outside. She was the clown on the street, the girl who stood dancing on the curb dressed in a polka dot costume, waving to the cars driving past, trying to attract enough attention to bring people into the high-end chocolate store where she worked. Her face was indistinguishable under white makeup, a huge red nose, oversized lips, and a Raggedy Ann wig. She looked like a freak, but as far as she knew, no one could tell who she was.

Finding a job had never been her idea. It had started two months before with the leather jacket she found on sale at Branson's.

"It's *so soft,*" she had moaned to her mother. "Like butter. And it's fitted, so it looks like a shirt almost, instead of a coat, and it would look good with almost anything because it's sort of a creamy color. You should see it on me. It's like it was *made* for me!"

"Believe me," her mother had answered,

"at that price it was *not* made for you. It was made for someone with lots of money."

"It could be for my birthday," Chelsea suggested hopefully.

"That's eight months away! And I don't spend that kind of money on birthday presents. If you want to buy yourself expensive clothes, Chelsea, then you'd best get off your behind and find yourself a job."

She gave it brief consideration but knew that by the time she had done her resume and gone job hunting, the jacket would be long gone from the rack. She went to Leanne and begged for a loan. Leanne had always been so good at saving her money. It had taken some groveling and some tears, and the promise that the jacket could be borrowed once or twice, but it was worth it, even though she now owed Leanne more money than she'd be able to repay in a year of weekly allowances.

After that, it was the hair incident.

"*How* much?" her mother had asked in horror.

"Seventy dollars. But it's worth it, Mom. Federico does the best cut of anyone in town and he can make my hair look way fuller than it does right now. I can hardly stand to look at myself sometimes." She ran her hands through her hair in disgust.

"Here's the deal, Chelsea." Her mother went to her wallet and pulled out fifteen dollars. "Here's what it'll cost to get your hair cut at Super Cuts. You can go there and get it done, or you can apply the fifteen toward the seventy dollar cut and find fifty-five dollars of your own to pay to Federico, who must be using golden scissors to make his services worth so much!"

"Super Cuts! Oh my God, Mom! Have you seen what they *do* to hair in there?"

"Better think about finding a job then."

Chelsea was left sitting in a chair staring at the fifteen dollars. She couldn't believe that her mother only gave her fifteen dollars for a haircut. She shuddered to think that it was barely enough to pay for the shampoo that she liked to buy from Federico's salon.

As much as she disliked the idea, she could see that a job was going to be necessary.

She put together a sparse resume and left it at all of the clothing stores where she normally shopped. There never seemed to be anyone over the age of twenty working there, and she suspected that they took her resume and tossed it into a garbage pail underneath the counter. When she didn't hear back from any of them, she announced to anyone who would listen that there were no jobs to be had in the city.

If it weren't for Jamal, she'd probably still be out of work, she remembered as she took her costume off the hanger in the storage room of The Chocolate Shoppe. She thought back to how frustrated she had been in her job search. She had met Jamal for lunch at the curry restaurant near their school.

"You'll have to buy this time," she had told him before they sat down. "I'm broke and I'm never going to find a job. There isn't one store in the mall that I haven't applied to. Without any experience, they don't even want to talk to me."

A short time later, after he had eaten a huge bite of his curried chicken and wiped his mouth on a napkin, he made a suggestion. "What about The Chocolate Shoppe? They have a sign in the window. Help Wanted –

Chelsea Davison – This Means You."

Her eyes had widened. "Really? That would be okay. I mean, it's better than a fast food place, right?"

He shrugged. "Whatever. It's a job."

She had taken her resume to The Chocolate Shoppe the next day, envisioning herself working behind the counter, sweetly serving love-struck men who were buying for their girlfriends, or small children who would point shyly at the candy of their choice. Instead, she had been handed a clown suit and a rubber nose. It had been tempting to tell Verna, the owner of the shop, just what she could do with her chocolate and the crappy job, but she had swallowed her pride, put on as much of the white makeup as possible and hoped for anonymity.

Then came the accident with her father's car. If she had harbored any hope of quitting work, it was squelched with the crushing of that fender. She was in so much debt now that this job was starting to look as if it would have to go on forever.

Chelsea pulled on her orange wig, looked at herself in the dusty mirror and sighed. Pushing her red rubber nose onto her face, she stuck her tongue out at herself and walked back into the store from the storage area.

"You look great," Verna said to her as she passed by the counter.

"Uh-huh," Chelsea answered, and she did a quick soft-shoe shuffle for effect as she reached for the front door and stepped out into the afternoon sun.

"Have fun out there!" Verna called to her before the door closed between them.

Chelsea took up her position by the street and tried to mentally prepare herself to begin. *I should find a job closer to home,* she thought, as she bounced without inspiration by the curb. *I can't keep slumming it on the bus. There's got to be a job near the house or near the school, even if it does mean working the counter at a fast food restaurant.*

The sky was getting cloudy. It was another downside of this crappy job, having to dance around in the rain. She looked up the street to the clock tower and saw the time was 3:50 p.m. More than two hours of work stretched ahead of her. One hundred and forty minutes of mind-numbing fun, one hundred and forty minutes of minimum wage.

A car horn beeped and she turned and saw Tara driving by with her younger brother. Chelsea waved and leaped around with exaggerated energy. It wouldn't last long, but it was a good show for a few minutes. Other drivers waved at her. They did a lot of that, waving and smiling at the clown, but it didn't mean they'd turn in and buy chocolate.

She felt something sticky on the bottom of her huge shoe and leaned against a light pole to check. Gum. She muttered an obscenity under her breath and tried scraping the shoe against the edge of the curb. *Definitely going to start looking for another job,* she thought.

But no sooner had she made the decision to change jobs when a reason for staying with this one came walking out of the pet store next door.

He was a hunk. Blond hair, broad shoulders, defined jaw, great smile, a butt to die for in those blue jeans. He was carrying a large bag of dog food over his shoulder and loading it into someone's trunk. She could almost imagine his muscles rippling under his black shirt with "Pets' World" stitched on the back. She had never seen him before so he must have just started working there. It was enough to make a girl want to buy a kitten or a bird or something.

For the next hour, Chelsea tried to keep an eye on the pet store while she was jumping around by the curb. He came out to the parking lot every now and again, helping someone with a heavy purchase. He looked great carrying that stuff out, so great that he made it hard for her to concentrate on dancing. On one of his trips outside, she became intrigued by the way his hair curled slightly at the nape of his neck. As she was imagining her fingers toying with the curls, she fell off the curb, right out into traffic. An oncoming car slammed on its brakes as she leaped back up onto the sidewalk. Chelsea turned quickly to see if the Incredible Hunk had noticed her clumsiness, but he was turned away from the road, speaking with his customer. A moment later, he was walking back into the store, and as she watched his every step, she made up her mind – she was going to keep this job forever!

A short while later, Chelsea was surprised and more than a little jealous to see her mother's car pulling into the parking lot with Leanne behind the wheel. But it was a good diversion, so she crossed the lot to the car with the exaggerated steps that her bulbous shoes created.

"What's up?" she asked Leanne as her sister pulled up to the front of The Chocolate Shop and lowered the window of their mother's car. Leanne was just eleven months younger than her. Other than having the same parents and having to wear matching clothes when they were little, they didn't have a whole lot in common. Leanne was shorter, darker, and, as much as Chelsea hated to admit it, smarter. She was in the chess club, the science club, the drama club, and the band. Chelsea stuck to volleyball and gymnastics. She and Leanne barely saw each other at school, which was pretty much the way they both wanted it.

"Just checking to see what time you're done with work. I'm getting my hair cut at five, but I can swing back and pick you up afterward if you want."

"I knew I was keeping you around for a reason! My feet are killing me, and I didn't want to walk to the bus stop." Chelsea looked at the Ford wistfully. She actually missed the old clunker, rattles, squealing fan belt, ugly turquoise color and all. "I'm done at six. Must be nice to have a car to drive."

"Darn right it's nice. And I'll get it more often because you won't be borrowing it." Leann was like that sometimes, sort of a rub-your-nose-in-it type of person.

"Wait'll *you* get in an accident!" The window was on its way up. "Or get a ticket! You wait and see! They'll be snatching that car out from under you so fast ..." The car was pulling away. She watched her sister stop at the exit sign, check both ways, and then pull out across the two lanes of traffic. She drove exactly the way they'd been taught in Driver's Ed. It made Chelsea want to puke.

She turned and walked unenthusiastically back to the curb, sighed, and tried to bounce a little. She started shifting from one foot to the other, waving listlessly at the traffic. Sometimes it was just hard to get into it. Being a clown was for, well, clowns.

The pet store guy came out again, this time climbing into the company's white van that they kept parked in front of the plaza. She watched him pull out of the parking lot. He swung right into the nearest lane of traffic and was about to drive past her. He looked over at her, grinned, and waved. She grinned back, which with those lips meant that her face was half covered in a huge red smile. For a second, she forgot she was in a costume. She hoped she looked good. She stared down the street after the van and forgot to dance.

She'd have to figure out a way to get his attention. *Sans* costume. No use trying to edge in on him while she was dressed like Bozo.

Before she knew it, it was six o'clock and Leanne was pulling the car carefully up to the curb. Chelsea walked awkwardly back into the store in her large shoes, quickly changed back into her own, said a quick good-bye to Verna and climbed into the car without bothering to change out of her costume. It occurred to her, as Leanne pointedly placed her hands in the ten o'clock and two o'clock positions on the wheel, that perhaps her sister could drive her where she needed to go each day. She'd have to find a way to convince her.

Chelsea chatted idly as they drove home, telling Leanne about the new employee at Pets' World and how he had made the afternoon almost bearable.

"So, are you going to talk to him?" Leanne asked her with interest.

"Of course I am. But not while I'm dressed like this." She pulled absent-mindedly on one of the pom-poms on the front of her baggy outfit.

"That's as good as you ever look," Leanne said and then ducked to avoid the punch that Chelsea swung to her arm. "Hey, you could have caused an accident!"

"Yeah, well it would have been *your* accident. Strike one." Chelsea looked out the window and watched as the local arena sign flashed the dates and times of the next few concerts lined up. "Hey, we're getting Avril Lavigne in May."

"I know. I've got tickets," Leanne said as she made the turn onto Payne Avenue.

"Really? Who are you going with?" Leanne's last boyfriend, Karl, had broken up with her three months earlier. It had been the worst. She'd cried for days and got really down on herself. It didn't help that he had ditched her for another girl. They all shared classes together. It wasn't good.

"I don't know yet. It's not until later this month. I'm just gonna hang onto them and see." Chelsea could tell that Leanne was being evasive.

Chelsea shook her head and looked at the houses as they passed by. Leanne was pathetic. She was hanging onto those darn tickets in the hope that Karl would be coming back to her. Poor kid couldn't tell when done was done.

"Your hair looks good," she told Leanne graciously as they climbed out of the car at home. Her sister wasn't as pretty as the girl Karl left her for, but she wasn't a complete loser either. *If she would just set her sights on the right type of guy,* Chelsea thought, *someone as average as she was, maybe she could find herself another boyfriend.*

"Thanks. I think it's too short."

If I'm nice enough to her, Chelsea thought, *maybe she'll give me a lift tomorrow.*

Heck, maybe she'll even take me to the concert with her.

"No, really," Chelsea said earnestly. "I doubt anyone will even notice that you had something done with it."

Leanne's body stiffened and her hand automatically flew up to touch her hair. Chelsea smiled at her generously as she passed her and went into the house. Sucking up in order to get a ride was going to take some effort, but it was worth it if it didn't mean having to face that bus.

Chapter 4

Two days later, after finishing work, Chelsea stepped down off the city bus and felt a spray of water splash across the back of her legs as the diesel-spewing vehicle pulled away through a large puddle. She pulled up the collar on her jacket against the heavy rain and ran the half block home from the bus stop.

"Here she is!" her father said cheerily from the kitchen as she came through the door, shaking water onto the mat in the hallway. He opened the oven door and pulled out a casserole dish with the chicken and rice he had made for supper.

"How was work?" her mother asked as

she put plates on the table.

"Look at me!" Chelsea moaned in response. "I'm soaked! I should be paid twice as much on days like this." Leanne grabbed a tea towel from the counter and tossed it to her with a grin. Chelsea patted her hair and wiped the rain from her face, leaving mascara smears on the cloth.

"Go and change. We'll wait for you," her mother said. "And put that towel in the hamper." Chelsea shivered and ran up the stairs to dry off and change into some warm clothes.

When she was comfortably dressed in a sweatshirt and her flannel pajama bottoms, she went downstairs and joined them at the table.

"Can anybody pick me up after school tomorrow?" Chelsea asked as she helped herself to the rice.

"I'm out of town," her mother answered. "I've got a trade show for the next few days."

"Dad?"

He shook his head. "I've got meetings most of the afternoon. I'll be lucky to get out of the office before seven."

She sighed and wondered if it was worth suggesting that she could drive him to work and then keep the car and pick him up later. He looked over at her and shook his head.

"Don't even think of suggesting it."

"I didn't!" she said resentfully. "I don't know how I'm supposed to get everywhere though. I've got a volleyball game over at Rydell, and I'm supposed to be at work at four, and there aren't any buses that will get me there without about a hundred transfers ..."

"Sorry. I know it's a struggle, but until you can afford to buy your own car ..." Despite the apology, her father's voice was less than sympathetic.

"Like that'll ever happen," she said under her breath. She poked at her rice with her fork and then looked as though she had just had an idea. "I know! Maybe Leanne could have the car for the day and drive me to the game and then to work. You could stay and watch my game," she suggested to Leanne enthusiastically.

"Oh, no," her father said with an amused chuckle. "No one is going to be inconvenienced in order to chauffeur you around town. Leanne doesn't get the car just for your benefit."

Chelsea sunk down in her chair in defeat. She was desperately trying to come up with an alternate strategy when the sound of the doorbell made her straighten in anticipation.

"I'll get it," Leanne said, pushing her chair back and heading for the front door. A moment later, Chelsea could hear voices approaching through the living room, and then Leanne was back, her hand leading someone into the kitchen.

"Everyone," she said, "you remember Denny."

"Of course," both parents said, smiling and looking not the least bit surprised to see Denny back in their house. Chelsea just stared at him, her mouth slightly gaping. What was Denny Waddell doing here again?

As if Leanne had read her mind, she said "We're going to the basketball game."

"Together?" Chelsea asked. It was a dumb question given that Denny was standing there with Leanne's hand on his arm.

"Yeah. What do you think, he came here to say hello and then go by himself?" Leanne reached across her chair and picked up her empty dishes.

"Actually, I was returning your dad's photography books too," he said casually, placing them on the countertop.

"Thanks!" Leanne answered, as though he had brought her some flowers.

"I'll do those dishes," her mother said to Leanne. "You two just go ahead and have fun. How have you been, Denny?"

"Good, thanks, Mrs. Davison." He was cleaned up, his hair washed and combed, his shirt tucked neatly into his jeans. Nothing different about the acne though. The guy was a walking science experiment.

"It's Fran. And John."

Denny nodded, but Chelsea figured he'd still call them Mr. and Mrs. Davison.

Leanne grabbed a jacket and stuck her wallet into the pocket before stepping into her shoes. "We don't want to be late."

"Have fun," her father said as he rose from the table. "Behave yourself."

Chelsea and Leanne both gave him a

look of disgust, Leanne because she was embarrassed to be talked to as if she was twelve, and Chelsea because she couldn't believe he would even *think* that her sister would be so desperate that she might not behave with Denny Waddell.

"He's a nice boy," Chelsea's mom was saying after they left the house. Chelsea walked to the side window and watched as they got into his car. They weren't touching. He didn't go around and help her in or anything. It wasn't like a real date. *He's using her*, she thought. *He's using my sister to get to me.*

His car started up with a roar. The muffler would be blowing sometime soon. She watched as they backed down the driveway and out of her sight. It was a crappy car. But it *was* a car. And it was his. The answer came to her suddenly, as though Denny Waddell had hit her full speed with his rusted set of wheels.

She smiled with satisfaction as she turned away from the window. Denny could be her chauffeur. She'd just have to find a way to make him come up with the idea himself in time for tomorrow's busy schedule.

Chapter 5

"Did you have a good time last night?" Chelsea asked Denny brightly when she saw him at school the next morning.

He was bent at his locker, digging out his chemistry text from under a pile of loose papers and old assignment books. He straightened and swung the door closed with a bang, then hooked his lock through the double slot and pushed it till it clicked.

"Sure. It was a good game. Went right till the last minute before we got the final two points that won it." He started walking toward his class. She fell into step beside him. Denny looked at her with a surprised expression, and she knew what he must be thinking. She had never shown any interest in walking to class with him before. This was a first.

"I hope you gave Leanne the play-by-play during the game. She doesn't like sports very much. In fact, I don't think she's ever been to a basketball game before." Chelsea looked reflective, as though she was trying to remember when her sister had ever been in a gym. "I love basketball. I like volleyball more though. In fact, I play on the school team. Did you know that?"

"Of course I know. I know everything about you," Denny snorted. She shivered. *He knows everything. How creepy, how Denny-like.*

"We've got a game today actually, over at Rydell. You should come," she suggested. They were almost at their class. "If you're interested, I mean," she said with just a hint of a knowing smile.

"You bet I am. I'd love to see you play." He leered at her. Somehow on Denny a leer looked more like a grimace.

"Great! I'll be taking the team bus over. But maybe I could meet you after the game."

"Sure," he said eagerly. "I could give

you a ride if you want."

"Yeah, sure," she replied with pleased surprise, as though she hadn't considered it before.

She could tell by the dopey expression on his face that he couldn't believe his luck. He was probably thrilled, thinking *Chelsea Davison is going to catch a ride with me.* After all the effort he had made to get her attention, he probably still hadn't thought that it was ever going to happen.

"I'll see you at the game then," he said as he paused at the door to their class and smiled at her gratefully.

Chelsea caught the amused grins of two boys who must have heard Denny's remark as they passed by in the classroom. She hoped they didn't think that she was actually making a date with him. Denny was still standing in the doorway and didn't appear to be in any hurry to move; she turned sideways to squeeze past him without letting any part of her body touch his.

Getting a ride to work had been easier than she thought that it would be. *But how,* she wondered, *can I leave the game with*

Denny without everyone thinking that I actually like him?

* * *

The volleyball game was going well. Rydell had a good team but someone mentioned that their best player was off with a sprained ankle and it appeared to be working to the advantage of Chelsea's team. They were two points ahead when she was rotated to a spot on the bench and looked up into the stands.

Denny was just coming in, his red and black striped rugby shirt striking a contrast with the clothes of the other students. *He might as well just wear a sign that says "GEEK,"* Chelsea thought. She watched as he stepped in front of someone to take an empty seat on the bleacher. As he sat down, her eyes focused on the boy sitting next to him. It was the guy from the pet store, here, at her game! For a brief moment, she wondered if he had come to watch her play, but then she told herself to get a grip and stop believing in fairy tales. He didn't even know her. He must be a Rydell student. She decided that she had better play her best game ever. Even if he didn't know her, she could still try to get his attention.

She let her eyes scan the remainder of the fans. There were several girls there she knew from her gymnastics team at Central High, as well as Jamal and a few of his friends. She waved to Jamal quickly as she returned to a position on the floor and got ready for the serve.

It was as though she had been injected with a dose of adrenaline. Her serves were perfect, her returns dead on. The team rallied together, caught up in Chelsea's energy, and came from behind to win by a narrow margin. The girls met in the middle of the floor to do high-fives and excitedly recount their best plays.

"You were awesome, Chelsea!" Tara said as she hugged her friend. "When I dove and missed that one smash, and you came from out of nowhere to recover ..."

"It felt good," Chelsea agreed. She glanced up into the stands to try and see if tall, blond, and handsome was still there.

Instead, she caught Denny staring at her, his mouth slightly open. She realized that all the sweating she had been doing had made her uniform top cling to her wetly. She pulled it away from her body and shook it a couple of times, letting air waft up to dry her.

She looked back up and saw Pet Shop Boy on the bottom bleacher step, pinned between a tall girl and a couple of younger girls who appeared to be vying for his attention.

"What are you guys doing now?" Sissy Rivera asked Chelsea and Tara as they filed into the visitor's change room.

"I have to go to work," Chelsea complained.

"I'm not doing anything," Tara said. "What did you have in mind?"

"A bunch of us are going to get the team bus to drop us off at the mall to shop, and then we're going to see an early show." Sissy peeled off her uniform and dug through her gym bag until she found her shampoo. "Do you want to come?"

"Sure! Can you call in sick or something, Chels? You should come with us."

Chelsea shook her head. "I can't. I already told Verna that I had a game and I'd be late. She'd know that I'm not really sick."

"How are you getting to work?" Tara asked. "There isn't a city bus route out here, is there?"

Chelsea hesitated. "I'm getting a ride."

Chelsea showered quickly and changed back into her school clothes, saying good-bye over her shoulder as she dashed out of the locker room. If she was lucky, she could beat the girls to the parking lot and avoid having them see her with Denny.

He was there, standing next to his old Chevy and watching the main doors of the school, apparently eager to see her step outside. Chelsea took a deep breath and started down the paved path toward the parking lot. A small group of students came out another door and headed toward her, laughing and jostling each other with familiarity.

Oh no, she thought in horror as she realized that her blond Adonis was heading toward her at the same time that Denny was walking from his car to meet her.

"Hey, Chels!" she heard from behind.

She turned and saw Jamal coming through the main doors of the school.

"Hi!" she called with relief, retracing her steps toward the school, away from Denny.

"Are you walking home?" Jamal asked her. "We'll walk with you if you don't mind being with these guys." He gestured toward his friends who were trying to trip each other on the steps.

Chelsea saw his eyes move past her and she turned and saw Denny come up behind her. Pet Shop Boy was getting closer, now just a few yards away. She grabbed Jamal's arm and kissed him lightly on the cheek.

"I'm so glad you came to watch the game," she gushed, clinging to his arm and walking him down to the parking lot. She put her head back and laughed as though he had just said something incredibly amusing, then leaned toward him and squeezed her face into his shoulder. "Just humor me, all right?" she hissed under her breath.

She led him over to the passenger side of Denny's car and leaned against it provocatively. "I'd love to go with you, but I already promised my sister's friend that he could drive me to work," she said effusively. She gestured toward Denny, who was following with a blank expression. "But I'll talk to you later on, all right?" She kissed his cheek again and got into the car with a flourish.

Denny climbed in and started the engine. As he pulled out of the parking spot, she glanced back and saw Tara and the girls looking at her from the steps, and Jamal standing in the parking lot with an amused grin.

"I have to go to work," she told Denny, as though she was talking to a taxi driver. She gave him the address and then thought to add, "Thanks."

As he dropped her off in front of the store, he turned to her with his brow furrowed. "Are you and Jamal like ... ?"

She thought quickly. If she said that Jamal was her boyfriend, then Denny might not be interested in driving her anywhere again. If she said he wasn't, then Denny might think *he* could be. She had to find a way to keep him interested without encouraging him too much.

"We're pretty close friends," she intimated. "But I'm not tied down. Thanks a lot for the ride."

"That's okay," he answered, looking pleased by her response. "Anytime."

He drove away, his muffler making it easy to follow his progress down the road.

Chelsea went inside and greeted Verna with a satisfied smile. She had planted the seed that could grow into a viable relationship with Denny and his car. Now all she had to do was figure out a way to keep it fertilized.

Chapter 6

At the end of the following week, Chelsea was working on the curb in the rain again. This may have been the worst month in the history of weather. Despite the elastic that gathered in the loose material of the legs of her clown costume, the material still hung down over her huge red shoes. It was soaking up the water from the puddles she was dancing through, making the glossy yellow and red material cling to her calves.

The only concession The Chocolate Shoppe made for bad weather was to hand her an umbrella on her way to the curb. "Hold this above you and use it like a prop," Verna told her. "Pretend you're Gene Kelly doing 'Singing in the Rain.' People will love it!"

People did love it. She looked like a drowned rat prancing around with an umbrella. *Dance and they will come,* she thought wryly.

All of a sudden, she heard a deep male voice behind her.

"Can I get you a coffee or something?"

It was him. The cute guy. The guy who could make the centerfold of *Playgirl*. He was looking at her with a half smile, his eyes saying that he felt sorry for her being stuck out here on the curb while cars splashed puddle water onto her legs, and that if he could he would pick her up and carry her away from this menial life and take her to a beach somewhere in the Caribbean or the Canary Islands where they could sip exotic drinks with tiny paper umbrellas in them, and do nothing more exerting than move their beach towels back into the sun when the shade of the palm trees threatened their tan lines. That is, if they even wore swim suits.

She smiled and hoped that her mascara wasn't running in the rain. *Oh my God,* she thought. *I'm worrying about mascara and I'm wearing a rubber nose.*

"That would be so nice," she said gratefully. "Just cream, no sugar."

"You got it," he said. She watched as he trotted off, circling around puddles as he crossed the parking lot to the coffee shop at the end of the plaza. Even through wet eyelashes, she could see that he had one truly fine rear view.

The rain suddenly seemed just a little less maddening. It had brought him over to her. It had given them a reason to speak. *Hallelujah!* she thought. *Bring it on!*

He was back just minutes later, passing a hot cup from his wet hands into her white-gloved ones. "I hope it's okay. I didn't know what size to get you, so I just got a medium."

"That's perfect." *Like you,* she thought. "I really needed this. Thanks."

"I thought you might need something. I don't know how you can stand being out here in this rain every day. I wouldn't want your job."

She held her umbrella a little higher and moved it forward a bit so that it covered his head. It was tilted slightly; the water started running off the back of it and dripping onto her neck. It didn't matter. She was already soaked.

"Even *I* don't want my job," she laughed. "But it's fine until I can find something else. I'd like to think there's something better out there somewhere." She looked into his eyes and wondered if he knew that *he* was the something better she had been looking for.

"There are only so many jobs," he said with an understanding tone as she nodded agreement. He looked back over his shoulder toward the store. "I'd better go. They just gave me a minute to run to the coffee shop." He turned away and prepared to head back into the rain from under the shelter of her umbrella.

"Yeah, well, thanks again for the coffee. I'd been hoping I'd meet you sometime," Chelsea confessed.

He looked surprised. "Yeah? Oh, by the way, it's Devon. Devon Bridgeman."

"Chelsea Davison." She looked at him shyly, but she was feeling anything but shy.

Give me some dry clothes, a little make-out music, and a back seat, she was thinking. *You have met the girl of your dreams, Devon Bridgeman.*

The rest of the afternoon felt much warmer, even if the rain never did stop. She spent the remainder of her shift in an upbeat mood, and despite the weather, she had to admit that for once she actually felt like dancing.

* * *

Denny picked her up at six that evening, arriving a few minutes early as he had for the past week. She had been speaking pleasantly with him every morning at school, convincing him that he was important to her while being careful to tell her friends that he meant next to nothing. "He's kind of like a brother," she had explained to Tara. "A creepy, ugly brother with a car."

She made small talk with him on the way home. What used to be an effort was becoming second nature to her now.

"Well, thanks, Denny," she said automatically as he pulled into her driveway. She got out of the car and looked at the wet imprint she had left behind. Her clown costume had soaked right through the worn seat material. "Oh jeez, look what I did to your car! Although maybe it's a good thing – it might actually clean the upholstery."

Denny's car was always filthy – paper cups and fast food bags were often lying on the floor when she got into the car. *He's lucky I even accepted rides with him,* she thought.

"No problem," he said brightly. "What time do you need to go to the mall tomorrow?"

"It's the weekend, so I'm going to a party tonight. Make it eleven o'clock so I can sleep in, okay?"

"Sure. See you then."

She swung the door shut and turned to go in the house without waiting to see if he waved good-bye. Leanne was standing inside the door with her hands on her hips. "Did Denny drive you home *again*?" Leanne asked accusingly. She moved to the side window of the living room to try and catch sight of the car leaving the driveway.

"You bet. He's my man!" Chelsea

laughed at her little joke. The idea of Denny being her man was too funny.

Leanne looked at her critically. "You are some piece of work."

"What's that supposed to mean?" Chelsea was honestly surprised.

"You're using him. Like he doesn't have any feelings or anything. Like he doesn't matter."

"Using him? Where did you get that idea?" Chelsea took off her shoes and looked at her feet, which were reddened from the cold rain. She should get hazard pay.

"Using him. As a chauffeur. The poor guy doesn't know what hit him. He thinks you actually like him. That you're interested in him."

"Well, yeah! Who wouldn't be interested in a hunk like Denny Waddell! I've been after him ever since I first saw his greasy hair and his single eyebrow."

She saw Leanne's face freeze, and it came to her like a bucket of cold water poured over her head. She stepped back and flattened herself against the wall in mock horror.

"Don't tell me that my sister is actually

interested in Denny Waddell? Oh, say it ain't so!" She laughed and unzipped her costume, peeling it off and standing in her turtleneck sweater and the tights that she always wore underneath. "Haven't you learned anything from me? Like good taste?"

"He's not so bad," Leanne said stiffly. "He's generous ... and kind of sweet, really. It's not that I'm *interested* in him. I just don't want to see him hurt by someone who's just using him as a personal taxi service."

"Oh, get over it, Leanne. He's getting what he wants – to spend time with me – and I'm getting what I want – rides to places I have to go. We're almost like friends. That's what friends do for each other." She bunched up the clown outfit and went into the laundry room at the end of the kitchen. Tossing the costume into the dryer, she set the time to forty minutes and pushed the ON button.

"That isn't what friends do at all, Chelsea. And you know it."

Chelsea frowned at her younger sister and shook her head. She had once thought that Leanne wanted to be just like her. Good looking, popular, and outgoing. What a laugh. Leanne wasn't at all like her. If her sister kept up that holier-than-thou attitude, she'd never get a boyfriend.

"You're so *moral,*" Chelsea said, as though it was an insult. She walked past her sister, ignoring the look of reproach that Leanne was giving her, and went to take a shower. She needed to relax and forget about the day. She was going to a party tonight and couldn't waste any more time listening to Leanne go on about poor beset-upon Denny. How could her sister actually like him?

She got into the shower and turned the hot water as high as she could stand it against her skin. As she squeezed the shampoo into her hand, she resolved that this was the last party that she would go to on her own. She needed to figure out how to get Devon Bridgeman to go out with her. From now on, she wanted Devon Bridgeman by her side, no matter what she had to do to get him there.

Chapter 7

The next day, Jamal was driving Chelsea home from the Y, where they had been shooting baskets together. "Come on, Jamal. Just swing by the pet shop for me. It'll only take a few minutes." Chelsea gave him a hopeful look.

"Okay, fine. But don't be too long. I have to be at work at five, and my mom wants the car back before I go," he said. He put on his left turn signal and slowed down when they got to the plaza.

"Thank you, thank you, thank you! You are such a good friend!" She grabbed her lip gloss out of her bag and pulled down the visor on the passenger side of the car.

"I might as well come in with you," he said, pulling into a parking spot.

"No! He'll think we're together." She gave him her "What are you, nuts?" look and pushed him gently against the door of the car.

"Duh! How could I be so stupid as to think you'd want anyone to know that we hang out together?" He laughed, but it sounded a little forced. "Oh, I know! It's because you hung all over me in the parking lot at Rydell."

She leaned over and kissed his cheek. "You're my bud, Jamal. You know I think you're the best!" And she did. "But we're not *together*. That was just so people wouldn't think I was with Denny. Stay here. Or go and buy some chocolate from my store. Here," she dug into her purse. "Here's some money. Get some of those peppermint ones and tell Verna that they're for me. She'll give you a discount."

He looked at her in amazement. "Gee, thanks, Mom! Three whole dollars!"

She stuck her tongue out at him and opened the car door. "Don't say I never gave you anything!"

She slammed the car door and walked toward the pet store, conscious of the form-fitting jeans and the clingy sweater that she had changed into after playing ball with Jamal.

She felt as if she was bouncing and glanced down to watch her chest. *Crap!* She was wearing a skimpy nylon bra that didn't have enough support to hold even a flat chest in place. It felt as if she could take an eye out if she walked too fast. She slowed down and inhaled to hold herself solid. Boobs. What a nuisance. Still, they did have a lot of power. These things could take you places.

When she got to the front of the pet store the door opened and hit her right in the chest. Wincing wasn't an option; Devon might be watching. A woman walked out with a child who was holding a tan and white hamster. The woman was loaded down with a cage, a hamster exercise ball, wood shavings, and pet food. Chelsea caught the door and held it as they moved out of the way.

"Good luck!" Chelsea smiled at her. Her own hamster had died when she was seven, the victim of a tragic blow dryer incident following a bath in the sink.

Devon was behind the counter, working the cash register. He looked up and gave her a quick hello as he rang in the purchase of another customer.

"Need help getting this to the car?" he asked the woman he was waiting on as he made change.

"No, I'm fine," she replied, grunting as she picked up the bag of dog food. He moved around the desk and opened the door for her, then came back and looked at Chelsea.

"Can I help you?" he asked. He could have been talking to anyone. An old lady. A ten-year-old.

"I don't know. *Can* you?" She smiled at him and pushed her bangs back from her face.

He looked confused.

"You probably don't recognize me. We met the other day." She tilted her head and wondered if he would remember her eyes. They were the only part of her that hadn't been disguised by the clown gear.

He studied her face, but she could see he had no idea where he may have met her.

"I'm sorry ..."

"Chelsea. I'm the clown," she said apologetically, because being a clown was something that required an apology.

His eyes lit up. "Chelsea? Wow. You clean up pretty good," he commented appreciatively as he looked her over.

"Thanks. You do too. Not that you needed cleaning up. I mean, you look good all the time." She couldn't believe she had said that. Thank God Jamal hadn't come into the store. He would have been choking by now.

"Thanks. Did you just come in to say hi or did you need something?" His eyebrows were raised, as if he knew the answer but wanted to hear it from her anyway.

"Well," she twisted back and forth a little, "I guess I could say that I came in for a cat toy or something, but then you'll come to my house one day and find I don't even have a cat ..."

He laughed and his face was beautiful. He was *so* good looking. He was Adonis. He was Jude Law. He was ... just *so hot*.

"I was wondering if you'd like to get together sometime. Maybe go for lunch or something." Her voice was hopeful.

He hesitated. She could almost feel her heart dropping as she waited for him to say something. *It's just lunch, for God's sake!* she thought. *It's not like I'm asking him to marry me.*

"I don't think that's a good idea," he said finally. "It isn't you or anything. I mean, you're really great and anyone would be lucky to go out with you, but I just – I'm not dating right now. I'm kind of taking a break."

"A break? From having fun?" She wrinkled her nose. "That sounds dull. What, do you just spend all your spare time playing video games and watching TV? Come on, everyone needs to go out sometime!" She tried her best to look appealing, pulling her shoulders back and tilting her head slightly. Rejection was not something she was willing to accept.

"You're making me sound boring!" he laughed. "It isn't that I never date at all, it's just that I ... there was this girl I saw for a long time. I'm just not used to casual dating, that's all."

"How about formal dating?" she teased.

A man approached from the back of the store carrying a bag of kitty litter. Chelsea stepped away from the counter and stood awkwardly as Devon rang in the purchase. She wondered if he expected that the discussion was finished, and she decided to back off for the moment.

"Well, if you change your mind, you know where I'll be." She nodded toward the parking lot. "Dancing up a storm, as always!"

He smiled, bagged the customer's kitty litter and waited until the man had left the store before saying, "If I change my mind, you're the first one I'll call." Her heart skipped a beat and she left the store with a satisfied smile.

She was conscious of her walk as she swayed her way back to the car with a breezy swing of her hair. When she jumped back into the passenger seat with a flourish, her cheeks were flushed and her eyes sparkled.

"I didn't nail it, but I definitely got him interested!" she announced to Jamal. She had too much pride to admit that Devon had turned her down for now. She was sure she could convince him to give up the celibacy routine and go out with her.

Jamal took a bite of chocolate and held out the rest for her. She leaned forward and took it from his fingers with her teeth.

"Does he know what he's getting into?" he asked as he turned the key in the ignition.

"What's that supposed to mean?" she asked absently, looking back at the pet store.

He shrugged and laughed hollowly. "Chels, you are not the easiest person to be involved with."

He stared straight ahead as he pulled away from the plaza. She adjusted the side mirror of his car so that she could catch a last glimpse of the shop. Devon could step outside for a moment and she wouldn't want to miss one last look at him.

She didn't talk to Jamal on the ride home. She was too preoccupied with the challenge that Devon Bridgeman was presenting. What was she supposed to do now?

Chapter 8

It was a simple plan, but sometimes the simple ones are the best. Starting that Monday after school, Chelsea began having Denny drop her off at work early enough that she could stand outside for a few minutes in her school clothes. Dressed in jeans and tight tops, she stood and window-shopped in the other stores near the pet shop, waving to Devon as she passed, as if she was surprised to find him inside. She never failed to speak to him when he did a heavy carry-out, and she had Verna tie ribbon around small packages of chocolates for him every day.

She had been heading into The

Chocolate Shoppe just before her shift one day when he opened the door of the pet store and called her name.

"Hi, Devon!" Chelsea answered eagerly, letting the door handle go and probably leaving Verna to wonder why she wasn't coming inside.

"I just wondered ... I thought you might like to go out for a coffee on Tuesday night." He looked uncomfortable, almost embarrassed by the suggestion.

"Sure. Sounds good." She wondered if anyone else in the world had eyes as blue as his. They were like a mountain lake on a sunny day.

"How about meeting at The Grinder's Café?" he suggested.

"Would you mind if we met somewhere closer to the west end of town?" she asked hopefully. "I don't have a car and it would save me worrying about transportation."

She tilted her head flirtingly and hoped he would offer to pick her up.

Devon looked slightly sheepish and shook his head. "It just works for me to meet you at Grinder's. If you can't make it ..."

"No, that's fine! I'll get there," she assured him.

"Maybe your brother will drive you," he suggested.

"My brother? Oh, Denny!" She laughed and looked down at her feet awkwardly. "Denny is just an old friend of the family. I wouldn't think to impose on him."

"Okay. Well, I'll see you there at seven-thirty, if that's all right."

"It's great," she assured him again. "See you there."

* * *

The days leading up until Tuesday passed by as slowly as a grandmother driving on a Sunday. Chelsea spent endless hours going through her wardrobe to find the perfect thing to wear for her date with Devon. In the end, she blew a week's pay on new jeans and a camisole.

"You look really nice," Denny said, admiring her new outfit when he picked her up for her date with Devon. "Are you going somewhere special?"

"Just meeting a friend." Chelsea thought for a moment about the possibility that Devon may see her climbing out of Denny's car in front of the café. "If you just drop me off at the corner of 5th and Brock, I can walk from there."

"Are you sure?"

"I've never been more sure," she murmured.

After Denny pulled over at the designated corner, she waited for him to drive off before walking briskly to The Grinder's. Devon was already seated at a small table near the front of the restaurant. He smiled and stood as she came across the room to greet him.

"Do you come to this place very often?" Chelsea asked him as she slid into the chair across from him. She glanced around the darkened room to see if she recognized anyone. She hoped that someone from school would be there to see her with such a good-looking date, but none of the faces in the café looked familiar.

"It's one of the places where we ... I like to spend time. They have great vanilla cappuccino. And the desserts are killer." He slipped off his brown leather jacket and hung it on the back of his chair, glancing over her shoulder and down the length of the room before sitting down.

Chelsea looked at his broad shoulders and felt herself wanting to reach across the table and touch him. *Stop it, stop it, stop it,* she told herself. He'll think you're an idiot if you start stroking his sleeves.

"Isn't a Grinder a hoochie dancer or a stripper or something?" Chelsea asked knowingly. "We aren't going to have some naked chick come over to dance on our table, are we?" She laughed at her suggestion.

Devon looked slightly puzzled before smiling slowly. "It's about the coffee. Coffee grinders, so you know it's fresh."

She blushed a little and concentrated on placing her napkin across her knee. "I know. I was trying to be funny. But if they served something stronger than coffee I might consider dancing on the table for you ..."

He laughed this time and she relaxed a bit. The café was trendy and popular; the small tables were almost all occupied and the long bar that ran along the restored brick sidewall of the restaurant was crowded with students and townies, the young working people who frequented the downtown eateries in the evening. There were small white lights clustered on hanging plants by each table, lighting the room enough to provide a warm atmosphere without the glare of lamps.

Devon waved and smiled at someone behind Chelsea. She turned to see if it was someone she knew. She didn't like being outside of her own circle.

The door opened then and a gust of cool air sent chills down her neck.

"Hey, Bree," she heard Devon say, and she looked closely at the attractive girl who turned at the sound of her name. The door closed behind her.

She was tall, very tall, when one was looking up at her from the small seat of a café chair. The soft mood lighting in the café made her flawless complexion glow warmly. Her hair was shockingly short, a tight, trim, perfect layer of curls that accentuated the huge brown eyes and the lashes that curled up to almost meet beautifully arched brows.

Her cheekbones were high, her makeup perfect, her legs long, her muscles defined and almost too big to be attractive. She looked remarkably like Serena Williams. She was smiling, her glossy lips exposing straight white teeth, her eyes softening as she looked straight past Chelsea at Devon.

She was with two friends; they murmured hello and looked at Chelsea and then at each other uncomfortably. Her friends left her lagging behind as they moved toward a table at the back of the room and joined a tall university-aged guy who was leaning back and watching Devon closely. Bree ignored them as she stopped next to Devon.

Chelsea turned back and looked at Devon who was looking up at Bree, who was looking back at him, and then looking down at Chelsea. It was the longest two seconds she could remember.

"Hey. I'm Chelsea," she said.

That seemed to trigger something in Devon because he leaned across the table and took her hand in his, squeezing her fingers as though she was falling off the chair and he was trying to keep her from hitting the floor.

"Yeah, this is Chelsea," he said defensively, his mouth smiling, but his jaw tight.

"Nice to meet you," the tall girl said, smiling genuinely at Chelsea, her long fingers undoing the buttons on her coat. "I didn't expect to see you here," she said to Devon, as though by way of explanation.

"No reason why we can't both be here," he assured her.

She smiled again, then looked at Chelsea's hand, which was starting to feel as though the blood flow may have been cut off.

"Didn't I see you playing volleyball a couple of weeks ago?" she asked Chelsea. "At Rydell?"

"Yeah, I play for Central." She realized that Bree was the girl she had seen with Devon at the end of the game.

"I usually play for Rydell, but I was coming off an injury," Bree explained. She looked back at her friends who were watching from their table. "I'd better go. We're just here for a quick snack before we go to a show. Glad to have run into you both. Have a nice time," she said, smiling easily at them before moving toward the back of the room.

Chelsea watched Devon's eyes follow the girl as she worked her way between the tables.

"Wow," Chelsea said, watching as Devon slumped slightly in his chair and released her hand. "I guess I should ask who that is, but I'm not sure I really want to know."

Devon waved to a waiter across the room and asked Chelsea what she wanted, placing their orders and waiting quietly as placemats and cutlery were laid carefully before them.

"That's Briana. My old girlfriend. It's been over for nearly a month."

Chelsea looked at his face doubtfully.

"Really. We're done. She's not right for me. She hardly ever had time for me and when we did finally get some time together, all we did was fight."

"Who broke up with who?" Chelsea asked pointedly.

He half laughed and looked down at the table, picking up his fork and toying with the tines.

"What difference does it make? It's over. Besides, she has another boyfriend already."

So she dumped you, Chelsea thought.

He put the fork down and took her hand again, gently this time. "I want to be here with you," he said reassuringly. "I like you, Chelsea. You're funny, and smart, and cute, and I want to spend time with you and get to know more about you."

She smiled. The conversation was definitely improving.

"I wouldn't be here with you unless I thought you were someone I could be serious about," he went on. "I'm not someone who dates a lot of different girls. I'm the kind of guy who gets committed to someone. I like serious relationships."

The waiter came back with two plates.

"Carrot cake?" he asked. Chelsea nodded and he laid it in front of her. "And a puffed pastry," he said, placing a plate in front of Devon.

For some reason, that struck them both as funny, and they laughed together comfortably. She tried not to notice when he glanced back at Bree repeatedly while they ate.

Chapter 9

The Thursday evening of the next week, Chelsea clutched her popcorn and leaned closely toward Devon. "I just don't believe it! That girl is everywhere we go!" she hissed.

They were in the back row of the theater, and Briana had just started up the aisle toward them with a boy carrying popcorn and drinks.

"This is the third time in a week! It's like she's following you," Chelsea said with more than a hint of annoyance.

"I don't think so, Chelsea. Besides, she didn't even see us."

They watched as she stopped a few

rows in front of them and spoke to her date, then edged past a few people to settle into seats in the middle of the row.

"That's just great," Chelsea moaned. "We get to look at the back of her head all through the show."

The lights dimmed and the first preview began.

"Don't worry about her," Devon whispered, his breath warm on her ear. "I'm here with you, and that's all that matters." He put his arm around her and squeezed her shoulder.

The movie was good, but Devon had to ask several times what was going on. Chelsea had noticed it before – Devon wasn't the sharpest tool in the shed. Still, he looked good and that was important when you were half of a couple.

When the movie ended and they stood to slip their jackets back on, Briana caught sight of them and waved. Devon waved back and made a point of helping Chelsea with her coat and then kissing her. *That'll show you, Wonder Woman,* Chelsea thought smugly. She kissed him back and gripped his arm possessively as they walked toward the lobby. She could feel Briana's eyes on them when they passed her and her boyfriend at the door.

It was only too obvious. Briana was stalking them. Chelsea was going to have to do something about that girl before she interfered any further in her relationship with Devon.

Chapter 10

On Monday afternoon, Chelsea went into work, and when her shift was done, she faced a far bigger problem than Devon's old girlfriend.

"Sorry, Chelsea. Having a clown just doesn't seem to be the draw we had hoped it would be. I don't think business really improved much by it at all." Verna looked tired and old. She obviously didn't like having to tell employees that they were being let go.

Chelsea pulled off the sponge nose. "So that's it then? I'm finished now?"

"Sorry, sweetie. I'll pay you another

week's wages, but you don't need to come in. I'll be happy to give you a reference."

"I'll bring the clown costume back tomorrow. I might as well wash it for you."

Chelsea felt bad, not just for herself but for Verna, who was obviously upset. "I liked working for you," Chelsea said. She had. Even though the job itself had been horrendous, Verna had been great. She had sent home a ton of chocolate for her family, and she had always understood if Chelsea had been forced to schedule her hours around volleyball practice and games. Where was she going to find another job like that?

Denny came to pick her up at six. When he pulled up, she was sitting on the step outside the store, toying with the pom-poms.

"Here, Chelsea," Verna said, leaning out of the open shop door as the car pulled up. "This is just a little something for you and your friend." She handed Chelsea a bag full of chocolate and smiled down at Denny when he stopped. He had been by the store so often that she probably thought he was Chelsea's boyfriend. Chelsea considered clarifying things, but decided it wasn't worth it now that the job was over. "I put in some of those peppermint ones that you like so much."

"Thanks, Verna. That was really nice of you." She hugged the older woman and stepped off the sidewalk to open the door to Denny's car. "I'll stop in and visit sometimes."

Chelsea slammed the door behind her, and Denny drove away slowly, looking at her dejected face.

"What happened?" he asked, pulling out onto the street. "Were you fired or something?"

"No, I got laid off." She pulled at the pom-pom again and it fell off in her hand. Perfect.

"Bummer. You should apply at the pizza place where I work. They'll be hiring for the summer soon."

She shook her head. "Pizza's greasy. It causes zits." Out of the corner of her eye, she saw Denny touch his forehead. "I want full time somewhere when school is done in June. I'm going to see if Dad can get me in at his company. They hire family for the summers sometimes. It would be boring and I'd have to work with Dad all day, but the pay would be good."

"Yeah, that sounds all right." He was quiet for a moment. "How's it going with that guy from the pet store?"

Her eyes lit up and she leaned toward him eagerly. "Oh my God, Denny. He is *so* wonderful! We've been seeing each other for a couple of weeks now and it's really working out."

He only hesitated for a second before saying, "That's great. I'm happy for you."

"There's only one thing that bugs me," she continued, looking out the window. "I mean, he's good looking, and he's so nice – I mean, he pays for every meal, every movie. But he has this ex-girlfriend who keeps showing up wherever we go. It's kind of creepy. She just hangs around watching him. I feel like she's a stalker or something."

She and Denny had spent so much time in the car together that talking to him now was like talking to a girlfriend. "Sounds like she wants him back. Does he still like her?" he asked.

"Like her? I don't know. They went out for almost three years. Three years! It's like they were married or something. I'm the first girl he's dated since they broke up."

"Transition girlfriend. Bad news," he said as he turned into her driveway.

It irritated her that Denny would suggest that. What could he know about transition girlfriends anyway? Besides, she had already thought of that. And she had done everything she needed to do to make sure that Devon couldn't just think of her as a transition. The last two times she had seen him, they had driven outside town to the gravel pits by the stock car track. They had steamed the windows up in no time, and she had worked his jeans off pretty smoothly, even if they *had* been fitted so tightly to that gorgeous body. He had stopped her for a second that first time, and asked her if she was sure she wanted to do this. It made him seem even sweeter than she already knew he was. She hadn't even bothered to answer him. The next night, he didn't have to ask. If sex could take his mind off his ex, then he should have amnesia when it comes to Briana now.

Denny shut off the car when they

arrived at Chelsea's house.

"What are you doing?" she asked him, as she saw him opening his door.

"Coming in. Leanne invited me to dinner."

"Oh." She was surprised. Leanne hadn't said anything about Denny since that talk a few weeks earlier.

She climbed out and followed him to the back door. Apparently he was a back door guy at her house now. He must be getting used to the place.

"Hi!" Leanne called as they walked in. She came over to the door and kissed him quickly on the cheek, then hugged him. She looked directly at Chelsea over his shoulder. *Got a problem with it?* Leanne's eyes were saying silently.

"There he is! Hi, Denny!" Chelsea's mom called from her vigil in front of the stove.

"Hi, Fran." *He's calling my mother Fran now. Wow.*

"I've just got to get changed. I'll be down in a minute," Chelsea said.

She trotted up the narrow stairs to her room. She picked up the phone and dialed

Devon's number. *Be home, be home, be home.* She sat down at her vanity and picked up a hairbrush. *Be home. Pick up.*

"Hello?"

"Who would you rather see tonight more than anyone else in the whole wide world?" she asked with a teasingly husky voice.

"Hmmm. Let's see. I guess I'd have to say Angelina Jolie would be my first pick."

She walked over to the bed and lay back on the pillow, looking up at the light on the wall above her head. A fly was buzzing around the bulb, whacking into it noisily and with annoying frequency.

"I'm sorry. Angelina's busy. I, however, would love nothing more than to get away from an evening with my sister and Denny, who apparently are now a bona fide creepy couple. Want to go to a movie or something?"

He didn't answer for just a moment. "I can't. I'm, uh, busy tonight." He sounded guilty, maybe even embarrassed.

"Oh." It wasn't what he had said. It was how he said it. She could tell that he was uncomfortable telling her he was busy. "What are you doing?"

He was quiet for a moment. Then he confessed, "I'm meeting Briana. Her grandmother died and she wants to talk."

"Oh." *Talk. She wants to talk. Talk, talk, talk. Got to talk. Nothing wrong with talking. Everyone needs to talk.*

"Why don't I call you later?" he suggested. "Will you be home later tonight?"

She sat up on the side of the bed. "I don't know. Probably not. I have other things I want to do." *Like hanging myself. Whatever.*

He didn't seem interested to know what that might be. "Okay. Well, I'll talk to you tomorrow, I guess."

"Sure." She had a hundred questions to ask him. "See you."

She hit the OFF button quickly and sat motionless, listening as the fly kept buzzing around the hot bulb. *Burn, you rotten insect. Land on the bulb and burn yourself till you drop dead!*

It whacked the bulb in frenzied confusion a few more times, then fell stunned onto the pillow beside her. She leaped up and flicked it onto the floor, then picked it up in a tissue and tossed it into the garbage. Good riddance.

If she could just get rid of Bree as easily. There was no doubt – she had to get rid of that girl somehow. And soon.

Chapter 11

The next evening, Tuesday, at The Grinder's, Chelsea excused herself from the booth she was sharing with Devon and walked to the back of the restaurant. She could barely believe that Bree was here again, at the same restaurant, on the same night that she and Devon were here. It was beyond annoying – it was psychotic. Besides, the girl's grandmother had just died! Shouldn't she be home mourning, rather than here hounding them?

Chelsea passed the door with a rooster painted boldly in the center and found the one with a matching chicken. Pushing it open and stepping inside, she glanced across and saw one stall door open, the other closed. Despite the availability, she stepped up to the sink and turned on the tap. She was there when the toilet flushed and Briana stepped out.

"Oh, hi," Bree said, appearing surprised, but not uncomfortable to find Chelsea in the washroom with her.

"Look, why are you always following us around?" Chelsea stood at the small sink and scrubbed her hands with the cheap pink soap that always filled the dispensers of restaurant washrooms. She was glaring into the mirror at Briana who had turned on the tap of the second sink next to her and was washing her hands.

Briana looked genuinely surprised, then laughed shortly.

"Don't accuse *me* of following *you* around," she said easily. "Devon knows my schedule. I go to The Grinder's every Tuesday at eight o'clock. I go the movies every Thursday. I meet my friends at the mall every Saturday morning. If you run into me at any of those places, you should know it's because *he* decided to take you there." She turned and hit the button on the hand dryer sharply, rubbing her hands quickly beneath the blowing air.

Chelsea felt her temperature rising. "Well, stop calling him. I know about last night. I'm sorry your grandmother died, but it doesn't mean you have to call *my* boyfriend. You must have other friends ..."

Briana shook her head in amazement. "My grandmother didn't die. Devon called *me* and said he wanted to talk. He's still got a thing, okay? Maybe he'll get over it, maybe he won't. Maybe he's not meant to. We'll see. But don't go accusing me of trying to move in on him. I don't need to go begging."

Briana grabbed her purse from the counter and took a last glance at herself in the mirror. She was striking, as always. She raised her arched eyebrows at Chelsea and smiled condescendingly before strutting out of the room.

The drier shut off, leaving the room silent and cold in the glare of the bare fluorescent bulb over the scratched mirror.

Devon had told her that he didn't care about Briana any more. He wouldn't have lied to her. Chelsea looked at herself in the mirror and took a deep breath. If what Briana said was true, and Devon really did still care for her, Chelsea Davison was not going to give up without a fight.

She pulled her lip gloss from her pocket and ran her finger gingerly through the cranberry-flavored gel, slid it across her lips and then added a touch to her cheeks to regain her color. Undoing one button on her shirt, she looked at herself critically in the mirror and was satisfied with what she saw.

She'd ask Devon if he wanted to go out to the gravel pit for a little fun. If there was one thing that Chelsea knew she could do better than anyone else, it was keep a boy's interest. And when she was done showing him why he was better off without Bree, she was sure he'd have no more interest in that girl.

Chapter 12

Friday night television was the worst, Chelsea decided. She was sitting alone, scanning aimlessly through the listings on the screen. She finally settled for watching *Grease* for about the hundredth time. Tossing the remote onto the table in front of her, she picked up her bowl of chips and curled her feet up beside her on the couch.

Her parents had gone away with friends for the weekend, and Leanne and Denny had gone to dinner and a movie. Tara and Sissy had invited her to go to some school dance, but she had said she wasn't interested. Instead, it had seemed to be a perfect opportunity to have Devon over to her empty house. By the time he had called and told her he was sick and needed to go to bed, it was too late to change her plans to anything but a night of television.

Her phone rang, and she flipped it open to look at the display screen. She recognized the number as Tara's.

"Hey, Tara," she answered happily, grateful for someone to talk to.

Tara's voice was urgent. "Sissy and I are at the dance over at Rydell. You have to get over here!"

Even though music was blaring in the background, Chelsea could hear that her friend's voice sounded strained.

"What's the matter?" Chelsea asked anxiously. "Are you okay?"

"*I'm* okay," Tara replied pointedly, "but *you* may not be. Devon is here."

"What?" Chelsea bolted up on the couch, nearly spilling the chips from their bowl.

"He's been talking to his ex for, like, ever. And now they're *slow* dancing!"

Chelsea's mind tried to process a dozen thoughts at once. She held the phone in front of her and stared at it as if it might tell her what to do.

"Chels? Chels?" She could hear Tara's voice from a distance.

"Yeah. Thanks for filling me in. I'm on my way," she heard herself say before she had even decided what she would do. She snapped the phone shut and, leaving the lights and television on and the chip bowl leaning at a precarious angle on the couch, went to the kitchen. Her mother's car keys hung from a hook by the back door. With only a moment's hesitation, she reached out and lifted them from the hook, closing her fingers around them with grim determination.

She arrived at the school in fewer than twenty minutes. There were no parking spots left in the lot, but she decided that it really didn't matter as she wouldn't be staying long anyway. She pulled up and double parked, blocking two cars, then grabbed her keys from the ignition and strode purposefully toward the doors.

"No jeans," a bespectacled girl inside the door said as Chelsea passed her without comment. "Hey! You have to pay me! And you don't meet the dress code!" the girl called after her helplessly.

"You made it!" Tara said excitedly, running over as Chelsea entered the gym. "I've been watching them the whole time. She's ditched her date – I saw him leave right after I called you. They've been out there just plastered to each other ..."

Chelsea was already walking away and was crossing the hardwood floor toward the tallest couple she could see under the movement of the red and blue beams of light that were constantly passing across the dancers. She ignored the questioning looks of the couples she pushed between as she approached Devon and Bree.

She stopped behind the pair and tapped Devon's arm. "Feeling better?" she asked, her voice dripping with sarcasm as she braced herself for an argument. Devon stepped guiltily back from Briana and raised his hands as though to hold Chelsea back.

"What do you think you're doing here?" Chelsea demanded. "With *her*!" She noticed Briana behind him and looked at the girl angrily, and then anger turned to horror as she recognized a look of pity on Bree's face. Pity! Chelsea Davison did not need anyone's pity, she said to herself with determination.

"There she is!" a voice said from behind her, and she felt a large hand on her shoulder. She turned and saw a middle-aged male teacher standing next to the girl she had blown by at the door.

"I'm afraid I'll have to ask you to leave," the man said, his eyes moving back and forth between Devon and Chelsea in anticipation of trouble.

"You didn't have to lie to me," Chelsea said to Devon, ignoring the growing group of people who had stopped dancing to watch them. "You've been cheating on me with *her* all this time, haven't you? I'm not blind."

"I won't ask you again, young lady," the teacher warned. "You have to leave now, or I'll ask one of the police officers to escort you out."

"I wasn't, Chelsea ... Bree and I *were* done. It's just that I still love her and I needed to get her back, and then you were there ..."

"So you *used* me? To make her jealous?" It all suddenly seemed so clear, the many times they had "run into" Bree on their dates and the way he had paid extra attention to Chelsea when he thought that Bree was watching.

"I'm really sorry, Chels ..." He reached toward her, his handsome face the picture of dejection, his brow creased, the gorgeous blue eyes slightly misted. Her own eyes narrowed in response.

"Save it for someone who cares," she said haughtily, and turned away from them, crossing the gymnasium with an entourage, including the teacher, the girl from the door, Tara, and half a dozen stragglers who were hoping to see a good fight break out. *Note to self,* she thought as she watched a path parting in front of her like the Red Sea. *Don't ever come to Rydell again because you are never going to live this one down!*

Tara hugged her arm as they crossed the parking lot.

"I can go home with you if you want some company," she offered. She looked at the car and saw Chelsea taking the keys from her pocket. "Your mom gave you the car?"

she asked with surprise.

"She's not home," Chelsea said by way of explanation. "I'd rather go home on my own. Thanks though. I just think I'd rather be by myself to regain my dignity." She smiled sheepishly and looked back at the school where a few people lingered outside watching her.

"Call me," Tara told her. Chelsea nodded and gave her a hug before slipping behind the wheel of the car.

She cried for a short time as she drove slowly home, but tears made driving difficult and took too much energy. She realized that anger was a far more satisfying emotion than hurt anyway, so she blew her nose at a stoplight and decided to stay angry for as long as it took to forget all about Devon Bridgeman and that smug girlfriend of his.

She was home in front of the TV before Olivia Newton-John had a chance to ditch the goodie-two-shoes act and turn cool. By the end of the movie, Chelsea had finished the bag of chips and was on her third chocolate chip cookie.

She heard Leanne and Denny pull into

the driveway shortly after midnight. They sat in the car for ages before coming into the house, giggling and talking in low tones together. There were periods of long silence. He finally left and the car rumbled its way down the drive.

"What are you still doing up?" Leanne asked when she came into the living room.

Chelsea was stretched out on the couch with a blanket over her legs, leaning up on a cushion and aiming the television remote at the set.

"I'm watching TV. What does it look like?" She flicked over a black and white movie, a late run of the news from the west coast, and an infomercial.

"Nothing on, huh?" Leanne fell into a chair beside her and swung her legs up over the arm. "Were you out tonight?"

"Nah. I didn't feel like going anywhere." She shut the TV off and tossed the remote onto the end table. "Maybe I'm coming down with something."

"What about Devon? Did he come over?"

Chelsea looked at her sister sharply. "I just said I feel crumby. Why would I want him to come over when I'm sick?"

Leanne held her hands up in mock protection. "Sorry! I just wondered, that's all."

"Yeah, well, he won't be coming over anymore. I broke up with him." She looked at her fingernails as though distracted, then added, "He was out tonight with his ex."

"Oh, no way! Do you know who she is?" Leanne looked at Chelsea with sympathy.

She shrugged. "I've met her. She was always hanging out at the same places we went. Her name is Briana Mobley. She looks like an athlete, all muscular and really tall."

"Briana Mobley? Are you kidding me? And Devon was dating *her*?" Leanne asked in disbelief.

Chelsea could feel herself losing patience. "Yeah. Briana Mobley. Why? What's so special about her?"

"Haven't you heard of her? She's training for the next Olympics. She's amazing! I saw her break the county record in the hundred meter run *and* the hurdles last year. Holy crap, Chels! Didn't you know that's who she was?" She looked at Chelsea in amazement and then started to laugh. "I swear, sometimes I think you live in a bubble. Did you try to take her on? Ha! Can you picture it? She'd squash you like a bug! She's probably stronger than Devon and Denny put together!"

"Well, yeah! Anybody would be stronger than Denny. The guy probably hasn't lifted a weight in his life!" Chelsea saw Leanne's smile fade and realized she had done it again. "I'm just kidding, Lee. Denny is really nice. He is. I like him."

"No you don't." Leanne swung out of the chair and headed for the kitchen. "I'm getting some juice. Do you want some?"

"No, I've been doing nothing but eating junk and drinking soda all night. I probably gained five pounds." She heard the fridge door open and the juice being poured. Leanne came back into the room sipping from one of the old juice glasses that had been taking up space in the cupboard for years. "I really do like Denny. He's been a real friend to me, driving me around and all," Chelsea said.

Leanne nodded. "Yes, he has. He's like that all the time. It's just who he is. He'd do anything for anyone, you know? It makes him kind of open to being taken advantage of. Some people don't appreciate just how sensitive and gentle ... and vulnerable he is."

"Ooh. Is that a dig at me? Because I might have been using him at first, but I'm not anymore. He *offers* to take me places. I don't ask."

"Oh, well then. That's totally different, isn't it? I mean, if you were *offering* to make out with Devon and he got it on with you every time you asked and then he turned around and said 'Oh, sorry! I didn't know you were actually doing that because you *liked* me!' Wouldn't you feel just a little bit used?"

Chelsea stared at her and tried to appear indignant, but it felt as if someone had just done a belly flop into her stomach juices. "What kind of stupid analogy is that?"

Leanne shrugged. "I'm just saying you should think of what your motives are. Denny is a really super guy and you hurt him. He's finally realized that you and he are never going to happen. And that's okay with him now because somewhere along the line he found out he liked me better than you anyway. Just don't count on all those car rides going on much longer because as much as he doesn't mind doing things to help you out, he isn't stupid. He knows that you're using him."

Chelsea turned the TV back on and came across a sit-com rerun. Watching it was better than looking at Leanne's earnest face.

"I'm really sorry about Devon being out with Briana tonight," Leanne went on. "He's a cool guy, and they probably have a lot in common, and a lot of history together too. It's kind of hard to compete with that."

She stood up and went back into the kitchen to rinse her glass. "I'm going to bed. See you in the morning."

Chelsea didn't answer. She had felt alone all evening. It was hard to believe that she could feel even more alone now. She had worked hard at this relationship with Devon. She had thrown herself at him, had sex with him even when she thought he might be thinking about Briana. She had given him all she had to give and it still wasn't enough.

She thought of Devon and allowed herself to be angry again. If she was going to get over Devon and avoid an endless stretch of Friday night reruns on television, she'd better quickly find herself a new boyfriend. And preferably, one with a car.

Chapter 13

If she stood back from it and dissected it all, watched the number of times they had walked into a restaurant and seen Bree, heard the number of times he mentioned her name, saw the way his eyes lit up when she came near, looked at the way his face appeared after she left, maybe she would have admitted to herself that she and Devon weren't going anywhere.

The morning after the dance, Devon called and asked if he could come over. He wanted to talk. Chelsea's response was deliberately cold and angry, but beneath her icy demeanor, her heart had leapt and her pulse was racing. He wanted to talk! He probably wanted to apologize, to explain that he had been a fool, to say that he had made a terrible mistake, to say that he loved her, and would never see Bree again. He wanted to talk. She agreed to see him that afternoon.

When he arrived, he wouldn't come in the house. She went outside to join him in his mother's car, parked by the curb in front of Chelsea's house. They had often ended dates this way, sitting and talking under the glow of the streetlights, but at those times they had been touching and holding and groping until she felt that she was at risk of her parents embarrassing her by flashing the porch light on and off as a signal to come in. Today was different. Today there was no touching.

He said all the wrong things – "I need Bree," "I miss her," "My life is tied to hers," "We're meant to be together," "We complete each other," "She is all I want in my life," "We're getting back together."

"So you were using me," she said to him angrily.

"Why would you say that? I thought we were having a good time together, that's all."

He leaned away from her, pressing against the car door. If he could have, she had the feeling he would have opened the door and run as far away from her as he could.

"You had sex with me. When you wanted her."

"That was your idea, not mine. You told me you wanted to." He looked hurt.

Chelsea bit her lip and took a deep breath. He was right. She had come on to him and had used sex as a reassurance that he was really hers. She had played all her cards to try and keep him from going back to Bree.

"But you were using me to get her back. You wanted her back, the whole time we were together ... you made sure she saw us together, everywhere ... you were showing me off."

He gripped the steering wheel and leaned forward in the darkness. She waited for him to say "no," that it hadn't been that way, that he would never have done that to her.

"Yeah, I guess I did. You were so pretty, and she was seeing that guy, and I was so jealous. I thought if I could just get her to see me with someone else, if I could make her feel what I was feeling ..." He sat back and turned to Chelsea. "I didn't realize that it would hurt you so much. I didn't know you could be sensitive. You've always seemed kind of ... I don't know ... tough."

She felt her chin rise slightly. Her lips twisted and then smiled. "Do you really think that *you* could hurt *me*?" she said. "I'd have to have cared a lot about you for that to happen. I'm not hurt, Devon. I'm just mad."

She grabbed her sweater from the seat beside her and opened the passenger door. "You weren't really ever right for me, you know. I need someone who can challenge me *intellectually* as well as physically, and, well, we both know that you're not the ..." She let the inference hang in the air. "Although, I must say, the physical was ... I can't complain about that ..." She leaned across and kissed him quickly on the cheek before climbing from the car. " Bye, Devon."

His eyes were *so* blue. She had loved looking into those clear, cool eyes. A person could fall in love with eyes like that.

"Yeah. See you."

She leaned over to give him one last

look, hoping that her cleavage showed to leave him with at least one regret. "By the way," she said, as though as an afterthought, "I saw how you dance and it was bad. Really bad. I can't believe any girl would dance with you in public."

She closed the car door, went into the house, and ran up to her room for a good, let it loose, the hell-with-swollen-eyes kind of cry.

Chapter 14

On Sunday evening, Chelsea found herself sitting in the living room under her father's glaring scrutiny. It was bad enough that she had been ruthlessly dumped, and that she had spent Saturday night totally alone and depressed. It was bad enough that she had spent Sunday afternoon watching Denny and Leanne cozying up on the couch together as though she didn't even exist, and that her life was stretching out in front of her like one long, boring, interminable wasteland of no driving, no dating, and no prospects. Now she had to contend with her father talking to her as if she was some sort of a prisoner who had broken parole.

"I checked the mileage before we left. The car has definitely been driven, despite our explicit instruction for you to *not* use the car." He waved a slip of paper in front of her.

"So you were testing me?" Chelsea answered defensively. "You trust me so little that you wrote down the mileage? I can't believe you would do that!" She shook her head in apparent disbelief.

"Of course I did!" he retorted. "And you proved to me that you really *can't* be trusted. All we asked was that you leave the car alone. Do we have to hide the keys from you?"

Chelsea's mother sat next to her on the couch. Her hand fell gently onto her daughter's shoulder and squeezed lightly. Chelsea knew that her mother was sympathizing because of the break-up with Devon a couple of nights before. Chelsea had told her about it, without the car details, as soon as they arrived home from their weekend out of town.

"It wasn't Chelsea who drove the car. It was me," Leanne said matter-of-factly, coming into the room from the kitchen with a couple of Cokes. She held out a cold can for

Chelsea, who took it with surprise, then walked to a chair across the room and opened her own.

"*You* drove the car?" their father asked doubtfully. "I thought you said that you had been out with Denny most of the weekend. Why weren't you in his car?"

"I just had some stuff to do yesterday on my own. I know I shouldn't have taken it without asking, but I didn't think you'd mind. I needed to get some, you know, *girl* things. That time of the month," she intimated, causing her father's face to turn red.

"Well, I suppose if it was an emergency ..." He turned toward Chelsea. "You shouldn't have tried to take the blame away from your sister like that. Leanne is a good driver and we obviously understand that these things can come up. You were about to be grounded for months."

"Sorry," Chelsea said with an air of relief.

"I'd better go and unpack," he told them, rising from his chair. He stopped and looked at Leanne's innocent expression, then turned to Chelsea who was leaning against her mother's shoulder. "Oh, sorry to hear about the boyfriend," he said kindly.

Chelsea smiled. "Thanks, Dad. There will be someone else."

"Of course there will," he assured her before leaving the room.

Chelsea looked across at Leanne and tried to thank her with her eyes. Leanne lifted her Coke in what Chelsea took to be a silent salute of sisterly conspiracy. They finally had something in common, she thought. Devon had turned out to be a lot like Leanne's old loser boyfriend.

* * *

"How are you this morning?" Chelsea's mother asked her sympathetically the following Sunday. Chelsea had spent the prior Friday and Saturday night home with her parents, which was torture for her. Two weekends in a row without anything to do was unheard of for her. Chelsea secretly promised herself that if her mother offered to play Scrabble with her one more time, she would throw the game away.

"I'm good!" Chelsea stated with false

confidence. "I've decided that I'm over Devon. I don't have to see him at the pet shop anymore, and he doesn't go to my school so I won't see him there. Out of sight, out of mind." She wished it was true. She wondered if she would ever fully trust a boyfriend's motives after this.

Her mother carried her toast and coffee over to the table and settled into a chair across from Chelsea, who was dressed in a crisply-pressed brown and tan uniform.

"I'm glad you're all right," her mother said with relief. "Because Leanne came home from the Avril Lavigne concert with a ring. Apparently, she and Denny are going steady."

"'Going steady'? Oh my God, who does that anymore?"

Chelsea's mother giggled. "I don't know. What do they call it then? He gave her a ring anyway, a little sapphire one. It's quite pretty."

Chelsea harrumphed as she got up to grab another glass of juice from the fridge.

"Too weird, my sister and Denny Waddell. I always thought of him as sort of a slug or a centipede or something. You know, an under-a-rock kind of insect."

"Chelsea! What a horrible thing to say!" Her mother looked at her as if she didn't know who she was.

"I don't really mean that. Well, I guess I do or I wouldn't have said it, but I meant I *used* to think that, back before I knew him better. I actually kind of like him now and I guess he's all right for Leanne."

"I should think so. He's a lovely boy. Very caring and kind. Exactly the kind of boy that I want for my daughter. It wouldn't hurt for you to find someone as nice as he is."

"Yeah, well, I'm working on finding someone, but believe me, it'll be someone better looking than Denny," Chelsea insisted.

She kissed her mother's cheek and pulled on a brown visor. "How do I look? Think I can pass for a dedicated coffee shop employee?" Her father's company had decided not to hire students, and Chelsea had resorted to applying to every fast food place in the area. She had started working at the coffee shop just the day before.

Fran stood in front of her and pushed the cap back slightly and straightened her collar for her. "I'll be in for a tea at about two.

Make sure you serve me promptly."

"Make sure you add to the tip jar!" Chelsea retorted. "I don't suppose you're heading out anywhere now, are you? Somewhere past the corner of Wellington and Main?" she said, looking hopeful.

"Sorry. I'm busy finishing up that report I have to have done tomorrow. Take the bus. You remember the bus, don't you?" She smiled at Chelsea's obvious dislike of public transportation. "It gets you right to the door. You're lucky. It could be far worse."

"I know, I know. I just wish the bus would take me somewhere other than where I'm going. I don't know how the heck I'll ever be able to save enough for a car when I'm earning next to nothing. And it's so busy in there! When they were training me yesterday, the line-up was right back to the door. I was better off as a clown!"

"Everything is relative, isn't it?" her mother said as she turned to wash the dishes.

Chelsea looked at her mother's back and made a face. Old sayings like that never helped her feel any better. She collected her things and headed out the door, reaching for coins from the bottom of her purse. *Got to have exact change,* she thought ruefully.

* * *

"Hey! You look pretty good in a uniform." Jamal was looking at her from across the counter in the coffee shop. He had stopped to see Chelsea in her new role as a server. "Not quite as good as you looked in a red nose, but ..."

"Very funny. May I help you, Sir?"

"Sure. I'll have a toasted bagel and a coffee."

"For here or to go?"

"Here."

"Black?"

"One sugar."

"And the bagel?"

"I'll have it to the side. On a plate would be good."

"Oh, you're just a riot, aren't you? What kind of bagel would you like?"

"What kinds do you have?"

"Whole wheat, white, sesame seed, pumpernickel, cinnamon and raisin, blueberry ..."

"Whole wheat."

"Why didn't you say so when I first mentioned it then?"

"I wanted to see if you knew what the other choices were."

"Anything else?"

"A donut, please."

"What kind?"

"What kind do you have?"

"Oh, come on! There are other people waiting to be served. I'm getting you a Chocolate Dip and you can choke on it for all I care!"

"Chelsea! I may have to put in a complaint about rude service!"

"Shove it."

"Shove it, Sir."

"Yeah."

She put his food onto a tray and took his money.

"A fifty? That's all you have?"

"Hey! I have a job that pays well. What can I say?"

She made a face and gathered his change.

"Thank you *so much* for coming in.

Have a nice day."

"Well, I'll certainly try. The highlight is having you waiting on me hand and foot." He smiled and picked up his tray.

She watched as he walked over to a table on the other side of the room. His jeans actually fit him pretty well. Darn well. In fact, Jamal was really looking good today.

She finished serving several more people and then grabbed a damp cloth and stepped out from behind the counter to clean the tables. As she got closer to Jamal, she smiled across at him and asked how his food was.

"It was good," he assured her, smiling as he watched her load the tray with dirty mugs.

"You know, Jamal, I've always thought you were pretty cute." She wiped the table next to him, taking care to remove the sticky residue from someone's spilled soup. "And I wouldn't mind if you and I were, you know, more than just good friends."

She moved across to his table, wiping the chair backs and trying to look busy as she judged his reaction to her suggestion.

"Oh yeah?" he said, half laughing as he looked across at her, eyes amused, his body leaning back and assessing her motives. "What do you consider better than just friends?"

She stopped wiping and stood with her hand on one hip. "Jeez, Jamal. Don't make me spell it out for you or anything! I just think you and I could maybe start seeing each other, like dating. It could be fun."

He laughed outright at this, his dark eyes flashing merrily. "Oh Chelsea, you are too funny. You know I've always been your friend, even when you've driven me crazy by ditching me for better offers or using me as a personal limo service. But if you think I'd consider dating you, then you'd better give your head a shake. You're a lot of fun, Chels, but you're too self-centered to have as a girlfriend."

Her face was blank as she listened. She thought she might have heard her shift leader calling to her from behind the counter, but she wasn't sure and she didn't care anyway. He was just a quasi-boss, a student who worked part time, like her.

"What do you mean, self-centered? I'm a great girlfriend. Ask ..."

"Ask Devon? Or Vinny? Or Ted or Cory? Where are they all today? Don't forget who you're talking to, Chelsea. I know you better than any of them, and I know you think about yourself and what you want first and foremost. Face it. I love you anyway, but if you think I'd ever go out with you and get caught up in a relationship any different than what we have right now, then you're delusional. Besides, if you had taken the time to ask anything about me, then you'd have known that I have a girlfriend already."

She looked at him doubtfully. "You do not! You'd have told me."

"You were pretty busy with Devon. Too busy for me. I've been seeing Cecile Desrochers for over a month."

Chelsea's face flushed, and she took his empty plate and added it to her loaded tray.

"That's great, Jamal. Really great. I like Cecile."

"Yeah, well maybe we can go to a movie together sometime. A bunch of us." He stood and added his mug to her tray. "I'm on my way over to her place now. Anyway, hope you like your new job."

She rolled her eyes and looked over at the counter to see her shift supervisor scowling at her. "It's work. It'll pay the bills."

"Yeah. I'll see you, Chels."

He headed between the tables and swung the glass door open. She watched as he walked across the parking lot to his car. His jeans had a small crease in the butt that shifted left and right with each step that he took. They really didn't fit that well at all. What on earth had she been thinking?

She carried the tray back behind the counter and resumed her position at the cash register. She wondered how many hours, how many weeks, how many months she would have to work to earn enough to buy a car – even just a rusty shit-box.

Her shift leader leaned past her to refill the creamer basket. The plastic tag on the front of his shirt identified him as "Duncan." He had freckled arms.

"So, Duncan," Chelsea asked, turning and leaning toward him with wide eyes, "do you normally drive to work?"